HARD EVIDENCE

Barbara D'Amato

HARD EVIDENCE
A CAT MARSALA MYSTERY

WHEELER
PUBLISHING, INC.
ROCKLAND, MA

★ AN AMERICAN COMPANY ★

Published in Large Print by arrangement with Simon & Schuster Inc. in the United States and Canada.

Wheeler Large Print Book Series.

Set in 16 pt Plantin.

Library of Congress Cataloging-in-Publication Data

Hard evidence.
    Hard evidence: a Cat Marsala mystery / Barbara D'Amato.
       p. (large print) cm.(Wheeler large print book series)
    ISBN 1-56895-861-7 (softcover)
    1. Marsala, Cat (Fictitious character)—Fiction. 2. Private investigators—Fiction. 3. Women detectives—Fiction. 4. Speciality stores—Fiction. 5. Chicago (Ill.)—Fiction. 6. Large type books. I. Title. II. Series

[PS3554.A4674 H345   2000]
813'.54—dc21   00-022866
                                                  CIP

ACKNOWLEDGMENTS

My thanks to Mary Lou Wright, of The Raven Bookstore, a mystery specialty bookstore in Lawrence, Kansas, for helpful research suggestions.

To Janice Kim for the Fern Ffolke and other ideas.

To Rita Rak for her mother's cookie recipe.

Thanks also to Brian D'Amato and Tony D'Amato for research suggestions.

Special thanks to Phillis Humphries for the use of her name and her profession. She is the sort of evidence technician you want on the case.

Thanks to Mark Zubro, mystery writer, for his person. And I should mention that the incident with the Chicago mystery writers is pure fiction. I have never met a group as mutually supportive and helpful as mystery writers.

To Susanne Kirk for the great osso buco dinner in Washington, D.C.

To Data Diggers, for digging data.

To Larry Bichelmeyer for showing me his meat department.

And thanks to the parrot breeder who did not want to be named. When I asked him for a certain fact about parrots, a fact that will become evident from reading the book, he said, "Maybe. You never know with parrots. They'll fool you every time."

Which is pretty much like people, I suppose.

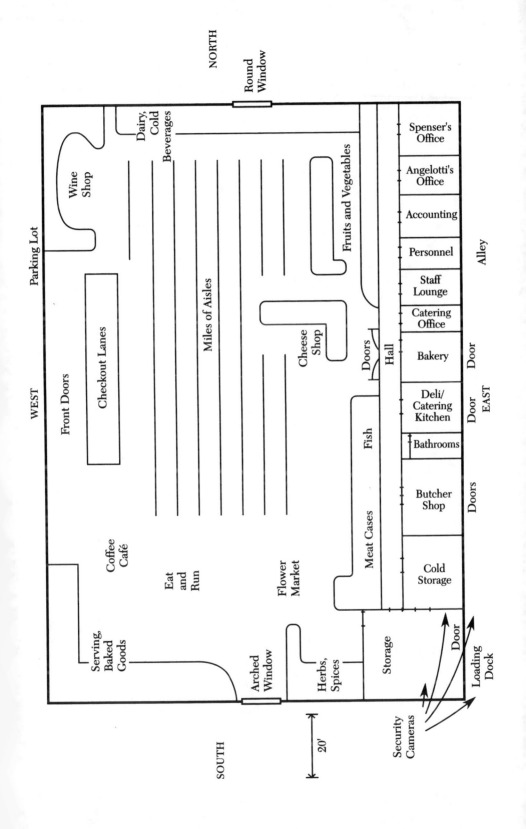

✧ 1 ✧

From *Notes on Food* by Bruno Angelotti:
"Osso buco is a specialty of Milan, in Lombardy, the northernmost part of Italy, where you find beautiful, serene Lake Como. The origins of osso buco are lost in the very distant past, but it can be traced as far back as the twelfth century in very much its present form."

I settled back on my secondhand sofa with a glass of wine and a feeling of utter peace. There's nothing more satisfying than putting in a day of hard work, in this case a morning of solid interviews for an article I was writing, interviews that wouldn't have to be done over again, and an afternoon of serious cooking. And then really kicking back with good company.

Sam felt the same, to judge by his body language. He was relaxed deep into the sofa as if dropped there, long legs sticking out, one big foot pointing north, the other south. Sam is a sweetheart. Very easygoing and accepting, he's a kind of Jimmy Stewart type, without quite so much aw-shucks. Maybe a kind of Nicolas Cage type—the Jimmy Stewart of the end of the twentieth century.

It's rare for Sam's schedule to coincide with mine. We've been semi-significant others for a year now, and if we've been able to spend seven whole days together or fifteen evenings, I'd like to know when.

He had just been in Atlanta at a conference on trauma surgery that had granted him four days' leave from the hospital but actually required only three away from Chicago. I had just finished a major article on the best restaurants in Chicago and was now "collecting quotes." The finishing touches. What you might call the garnish, the parsley and lemon wedge.

So he was spending the afternoon and evening at my apartment. This was better than nice. Onion soup simmered slowly on the stove. In the oven lasagna with meat sauce bubbled and roiled. You need five cheeses to make a perfect lasagna—mozzarella and Scamorze for the stringy layers, ricotta for the creamy layers, and Parmesan and Romano mezzo-mezzo for the top. And don't let anybody tell you different.

"I found some beautiful smoked salmon, too," I said to Sam. "Are you ready for your appetizer?"

"I think I could force myself."

All my ingredients had been purchased at Spenser and Angelotti, Chicago's biggest and best purveyor of foodstuffs. It's not just a grocery, it's a deli. It's not just a deli, it's a meat and fish market. It's not just a meat and fish market, it's a caterer. It's not just a caterer, it's an herb consultant. A wine shop.

A greengrocers. Spenser and Angelotti is a Chicago resource. I had done an article on the store six months earlier, and from the minute I walked in, I didn't want to leave.

The lovely salmon I now brought to Sam had been suggested by Bruno Angelotti himself. "Fine salmon. It's Norwegian, about a third less costly than Scottish, but every bit as good, in its own way. Very delicate flavor," he said. "Offer capers with it."

I poured Sam a little more wine and settled back into the sofa feeling that life was good.

The only fly in the ointment chose that moment to come ambling in. My best friend, Hermione, had gone away for two days to the wedding of her brother in Cedar Rapids and I was baby-sitting her eight-month-old Dalmatian.

The dog wouldn't have been such a problem except that my roommate hated him. My roommate is an African gray parrot named Long John Silver. Long John is the senior member of the household. We think he is about forty-five years old. LJ was brought to Chicago by the captain of a New Orleans shrimp trawler, a man who retired to Chicago after decades on the Gulf of Mexico, thinking there was no water here. Imagine his surprise when he found out Lake Michigan was so big you couldn't see across it.

The captain died a few years later and left LJ to a second man, an English professor who taught at Northwestern and lived in this apartment building. The professor specialized in Shakespeare. He owned LJ for twenty years. When the prof left Chicago, he left me the bird, so now I have a Shakespeare-quoting parrot.

LJ hates pets. To LJ pets are dirty, furry things with four feet. He has two feet and is not a pet. If not exactly human, he's better than human.

LJ had been scolding Dapper all day. Occasionally, when he thought I wasn't watching, he would dive-bomb Dapper, giving his ears a little tweak with his claws, and then fly up to sit on a curtain rod, saying, "Out, out damned spot."

"I felt so sorry for Dapper," I said to Sam, "that I bought him something."

"Why is one of his ears going bald?"

"Oh, no! Hermione will be devastated. LJ! If you don't stop, you're going in your cage!"

He stared at me and said, "Braaaaaaaak!"

"Dapper, let me get your surprise."

Dapper opened his big brown eyes, lolled a long pink tongue that resembled Canadian bacon, and said nothing. LJ fixed a scornful left eye on Dapper, then turned his head a hundred and eighty degrees to the right eye and fixed that one on Dapper. You could see him think, "Can't fly. Can't even talk. Useless."

I brought in the treat. "Look at this, Dapper! Bought you a treat at Spenser and Angelotti," I said, proud of myself.

"Mmmm. Look at that, Dapper," Sam said helpfully.

"Big soup bone, Dapper, just for you. Good boy."

I set the beautiful big end-bone down on

the wooden floor. It didn't have enough fat on it to mess up the floor much, but I don't have rugs anyway, because of LJ. I guess you'd say mine was a wildlife-centered home.

Dapper bounded to the bone. His eyes said, "For me?" but he didn't wait for an answer. He placed a paw on either side of the wonderful thing, grabbed it in his teeth, and sank down blissfully, surrounding the bone. No predators were going to get it away from him.

I relaxed back onto the sofa.

"Just a minute," Sam said.

"Just a minute what?"

"Let me see that."

He got up and went to the bone. He said, "Will Dapper bite me?"

"If you take the bone away? He ought to. But he probably won't. Dapper is a big pussycat. Pardon the expression, Dapper."

Sam reached down. "There, there, Dapper. Just a minute."

Sam snatched away the bone. Dapper sat up, shocked and sad. What was this? How could life be so cruel?

Sam held the bone, turning it in his hand.

"Um—I hate to tell you this."

"What?"

"We've got a problem here. We're gonna have to call the police."

✧ 2 ✧

"Select from a display of veal shins several good, large bones with sufficient meat on them."

"Oh, my God!" Bruno Angelotti said. "Oh, my God! Oh, my God!"

I patted him on the shoulder, which didn't seem to help. I was careful not to let him see that I was trembling. He was worried, but my guess was he didn't have a clue about how unpleasant this could become. Angelotti is a truly sweet man, and an artist in his own area, food. Writing the article on Spenser and Angelotti's I had found him lovable. People who have boundless enthusiasm are likable to begin with. His love of wonderful foodstuffs, great recipes, and his desire to share his love with everybody he met, made him genuinely adorable.

We were marooned in the lecture room in the Cook County medical examiner's office, with the clock getting on to 11 P.M. Bruno's partner, Henry Spenser, paced back and forth across the large room, trailed by a man in a three-piece midnight-blue suit that said "lawyer."

I left Angelotti and went to sit with Sam. "Sorry about the dinner," I said. "I mean, the first time we get a moment to relax, just the two of us, look what happens."

"Not your fault."

"Still. I'm sorry. And I feel so sorry for Bruno. Look at him. I brought disaster on him."

"Well, you couldn't exactly hide it." Sam put his arm around my shoulders. "Don't be responsible for the whole world."

"There are some really hideous implications here. Sooner or later, it's going to hit them. Actually, I'm pretty much upset myself," I added, thinking about my lasagna.

"I can see that."

"You're not supposed to notice. I'm supposed to be superwoman."

"No, you're not. You're supposed to be human."

"If I picture what may have happened, I feel queasy."

"I can imagine. You feel chilled, too."

"How do you know that?"

"Beads of sweat along your hairline."

"Well, just *think about* what may have happened."

"I have."

"Easy for you. You deal with human body parts every day."

"Yes, I do. But I'm aware most other people don't. Sometimes, though, people just have to face facts."

"Again, easy for you to say."

He pulled me close, shoulder to shoulder for a few seconds. "When we get done here, I'd like to go back and console you, but there's a work problem."

"There usually is," I said grimly.

"I have first shift tomorrow." This meant he had to be at the hospital trauma center by 7 A.M. Sam is a trauma surgeon. "I shouldn't operate without sleep."

"You're right." I sighed. The one evening we get together and this happens. Then I thought, how selfish of me. Someone has probably been murdered, and here I'm worrying about my date. Have a heart, Marsala.

"People's lives depend on you, Sam. You have to be responsible."

"Damn shame, though, isn't it?"

"A damn shame."

The lecture room at the medical examiner's office is very plain, with blank walls and molded plastic chairs that would be right at home in a high school lunchroom. Angelotti started pacing around the outside of the room while Spenser paced in short bursts up and down the middle, and we all waited for word about the bone.

"Why are they taking so long?" Angelotti asked, from the back corner.

We'd been here more than an hour. I said, "They aren't going to have any test results tonight, are they?"

Sam said, "DNA takes weeks. Drug testing takes days. No, they're just doing measurements. And an antiserum thing."

I said, "Which is what?"

"You add a specific antigen and if the blood clumps, it's human."

Henry Spenser turned a hard look on Sam. "Doctor," he said with an undertone of anger,

"I surely hope you're wrong about this god-damn bone."

"I hope I am, too," Sam said mildly. He deals with victims of very serious accidents and, of course, the victims' distraught relatives at the Northwestern University Hospital Level One Trauma Unit in Chicago. A little emotion in the air around him doesn't get him riled up.

"Suppose it's just a joke?" Spenser said hopefully.

"What kind of joke?" Sam asked.

"Like a medical student joke. A bone from a cadaver leg."

I said, "Who was supposed to *get* the joke?"

The door opened. Three men strode in. First was my friend, Harold McCoo, chief of detectives of the Chicago Police Department. I had called him immediately, knowing this could be serious. McCoo is a stately black man of about fifty-five, with heavy shoulders and a more portly midsection than he would wish. His wife, Susanne, keeps trying to slim him down.

Second through the door was Dr. Donald Washington, chief medical examiner of the city of Chicago. Washington is very tall, rather stooped, and thin as a stork.

Last was Dr. Thelonius Morgan, director of the health department.

They all looked serious. Bruno Angelotti came hurrying to the front of the room. "What? *What?*" he said.

Washington said, "The bone is human."

9

"Oh, my God!" Angelotti slapped his cheeks with both hands at once, a very Italian gesture.

McCoo said, "Let's all sit down."

We pulled the plastic chairs into a circle. Bruno Angelotti was still making little groaning noises, and the lawyer, whom Spenser introduced as William Barkley, frowned at everyone.

Barkley said, "Let me get one thing straight."

"All right," McCoo said.

"As I understand it, in this room as of this minute are all the people who know about the um, the um, situation." He gestured. "Mr. Spenser, Mr. Angelotti, Dr. Washington, Dr. Morgan, Dr. Davidian, Ms. Marsala, and you and me."

McCoo said, "Yes."

"Good. I would like to suggest—"

McCoo said, "So far. You're going to have to institute a recall. The city will have to know."

Angelotti said, "Oh, my God!"

"Now wait a minute," Barkley said. "You'd better be damn careful. You could destroy Mr. Angelotti's and Mr. Spenser's entire business with one ill-considered word."

"Mr. Barkley, don't get huffy. We'll take this one step at a time. Ordinarily I would have to notify Operations Command, but I'm ADS tonight, acting deputy superintendent. Nevertheless, there are two people who have to know right now."

"Who?"

"The superintendent of police and the mayor."

Everyone was silent. Even Angelotti. McCoo went on.

"I have a call in to both of them. The mayor is at the opera. The superintendent we're still tracking down. Let's review while we wait."

Seven pairs of eyes gazed at him.

"This afternoon, Saturday, Ms. Marsala went to Spenser and Angelotti's and bought ingredients for dinner. Among her purchases was a soup bone which she bought to give her dog."

I was going to say it's not my dog, but what difference did that make?

"This was a large bone, often called a knucklebone, even though they are really the ends of long bones. This evening at about eight P.M. Dr. Sam Davidian recognized the bone as human. Miss Marsala quite properly called me. Right? Okay, Dr. Washington, please describe the bone."

"Uh—it is the distal end of the right femur, which basically means here." He pointed to his upper leg, just above the knee. "It's the lower end of the largest bone in the human body. And this one belonged to a fairly large adult person, probably male."

McCoo said, "Thank you. Now. We have two problems, and they are entirely separate. First, we have to assume that the person this bone was part of is dead. We have to treat this as a homicide unless or until we find out otherwise. To put it briefly, it is my job to track down a murderer."

11

Angelotti groaned.

"The second problem is a public health problem. How did that bone get in the refrigerator case, are there any more human bones in the case, were any others sold, and were any other, uh, body parts sold?"

"Oh, my God!" Angelotti said.

"We can't assume that," Barkley said.

"Oh, yes, we can, sir. And for the time being we have to. Where there was one human bone there were probably more. We are *going to* assume that a person was dismembered in Spenser and Angelotti's, and at least part of that person found his way into the meat case."

Angelotti stared with his mouth open, too horrified to speak.

McCoo said, "Dr. Morgan, explain the public health implications."

"I have to say, I've never faced such a thing before. There should be no problems at all in terms of spreading disease if the material has been, ah, cooked. But I'm going to have to do some research to get a handle on this. It's just never, ever come up. Ever. Fortunately."

"Now, for the purposes of finding a killer," McCoo said, "I need as much evidence as I can get. For the purposes of safeguarding the public, we need to recall all suspicious meat. Which means informing the public. From both points of view, our first job is to pull everything off the shelves that could be part of the person—everything suspicious."

"Actually, I anticipated this," Henry Spenser said. "I shut down the store, which closed to

12

the public at ten P.M. anyway, and sent home all employees who would otherwise be cleaning up."

"Very good."

At Spenser and Angelotti, Angelotti was the man with the palate; Spenser was the man with the pencil. While Angelotti chose the finest foods, scoured the world, tasted the new star fruit and salad dressings and capers and Japanese beef, Spenser watched the bottom line, set prices, and handled advertising.

Obviously, he was the practical one.

"So," McCoo said, "evidence techs will leave from the crime lab within minutes to go to Spenser and Angelotti. They will collect all discarded paper and trash, take samples throughout the store, particularly in the butcher shop, fingerprint the area, and they will remove for testing all bones, plus all beef, veal, lamb, and pork."

"Do you realize the losses we're going to suffer?" Spenser asked. "We have three *tons* of meat in our cases at any given time!"

"It's going to get worse, Mr. Spenser. We are going to have to announce the recall on the morning media of all the meat sold recently."

"I—that's—impossible! It will cost us a fortune!"

"And that," McCoo went on, "isn't all. The decision has to be made about exactly what we're going to tell the public."

"Hold it!" The lawyer jumped to his feet. "You can't tell the public that Spenser and Angelotti has been selling—has been selling human—has been—what you'd do is destroy the business. They might as well *close*! This exceeds your authority."

"Sit down, Mr. Barkley. Thank you. This is not an adversary proceeding. I am not exceeding my authority. I could pull Spenser and Angelotti's food purveyor's license as of this moment. Then you'd have to go to the commission to get it back. The commission meets only once every two weeks. And I can assure you, closing Spenser and Angelotti does not exceed the authority of the mayor and the health department. This is a decision you will not make; they will."

Spenser said, "If it would help, I have a suggestion."

"Go ahead."

"Your goal is twofold. One: Get the evidence back. Two: Prevent any health problems. I want to make this offer. Tell the public there has been some sort of accidental contamination. Tell the public, please, that it wasn't the fault of Spenser and Angelotti's?"

"I think—"

"And then tell them that any beef, pork, lamb, or veal they bring back will be replaced either by products worth five times as much or by five times the price in actual hard cash! I'll go that high if it'll keep this mess out of the media."

McCoo said, "Mmmp. That might help. Miss Marsala was astute enough to bring in the wrapping from the bone. Going by the date, it was packaged Saturday, today. If so, and if we can be *sure* of it, we may only have to recall, say, two days' worth. Friday's and Saturday's. In that case you may not have such a huge number of returns. Anyway, we'll see what the mayor says."

"Because, otherwise you may utterly destroy our business."

"We'll see what the mayor says. But I don't believe in secrecy in a situation like this."

"His wife shops with us," Spenser said. McCoo merely rolled his eyes.

"And another thing," Barkley said.

"What?"

Pointing at me, he said, "This woman is a reporter. This unfortunate incident could be a real scoop. She could do disgusting human-interest pieces on it. It could be the story of a lifetime for her."

"This isn't the kind of story I do," I snapped at him, annoyed.

"You say that now," Spenser said.

"Plus, I met Mr. Angelotti when I did the story on Spenser and Angelotti last October. I consider him a friend. I wouldn't hurt him."

Spenser said, "You say that now."

"And I'll say it tomorrow!"

McCoo said, "Mr. Barkley, Mr. Spenser, give it a rest. You're lucky it's Ms. Marsala who found that bone. Although, I suppose you wish no one had. Or that no one had recognized it. Don't make me think, Mr. Spenser, that if you had known what the bone was, you'd have thrown it in the trash and never told a soul. Keep me thinking you would have behaved like a good citizen."

Silence.

McCoo's cell phone beeped. "Chief McCoo," he said into it, standing up. "Oh, yes. Yes, Superintendent." He mouthed "conference call" at us, and moved away.

"Yes, Mr. Mayor," he said.

He walked out the door into the hall and we couldn't hear any more.

The tension in the lecture room was terrible. Poor Angelotti sat frozen, his hands curled in his lap. Spenser's face was drawn. Even Morgan, the health department doctor, looked deeply worried. I could imagine that it would be horrible trying to explain this to the hordes of ravenous media reps who would descend on him if this became public.

We waited and waited and waited. McCoo would have to explain to the mayor, and to the police superintendent, every fact over and over and in detail. The superintendent was no forensic pathologist, and the mayor was a people person, not a techie in the least. Plus, both of them would be trying to figure the political fallout.

We waited some more. Just when I thought Bruno Angelotti was going to have a heart attack, McCoo came back, snapping his cell phone together. I knew he was angry because I know him well. To the others he probably looked businesslike. McCoo has never liked politics and he doesn't like cover-ups.

"We have twenty-four hours," he said.

"To do what?" Angelotti breathed, just above a whisper.

"They don't want to panic the public. Dr. Morgan will make a simple public health announcement. So will you. You may call the city news bureau yourself if you like. Everybody needs to get this with the morning news. Say that it's some form of contamination. They want you to be sure to say nonfatal or the announcement itself will cause panic. You"—he pointed at Spenser—"will give products or cash back as you promised. And my job is to find out what happened, when it happened, and arrest a killer. So let's go."

I said, "Wait a minute." Everybody stared at me, especially Barkley, the lawyer. You could almost hear him thinking, "How come she gets to talk?"

"Calling it a contaminant won't work because it sounds accidental," I said. "When your detectives start trying to find the killer they're going to have to ask the staff who saw who where and whether a stranger was hanging around the store and whether one butcher hated another butcher, and so on."

"You're right," McCoo said.

"But you could call it sabotage. That would probably allow for just about any kind of question. Grudges against Spenser and Angelotti, lights on in the store late at night, intrastaff warfare, everything."

Spenser said, "Yes."

Barkley grudgingly said, "She's right."

Angelotti, however, was still back at the decision to keep the reason quiet. With hope in his voice, almost unable to believe it, he said, "And they're not going to tell what happened?"

"Dr. Washington is to do the analyses himself. One reliable person on his staff will be chosen to help him. The evidence techs will be sworn to secrecy. Two teams of two senior detectives will have to be put in the picture, of course, but we'll tell them the mayor is very serious about confidentiality. Otherwise, only we here know. If you keep quiet—"

Angelotti said, "Thank you, Lord."

As we walked out, Spenser turned to Barkley and said, "Insurance has to cover this, right?"

✧ 3 ✧

"Saw—do *not* chop or crack—the veal shinbones into two- to three-inch pieces."

Midnight.

The store was cavernous and silent. Like all public buildings when the public is gone, it sounded hollow and felt populated by ghosts. The tail of my eye kept trying to catch a hint of phantom shoppers moving past the end of dim aisles.

In this case maybe there was a ghost. Certainly if a funeral puts the deceased "to rest" then whoever had died here was not at rest.

18

And yet, however echoing and ominous, this was a beautiful store. A U.S.-style supermarket is a huge bazaar, bigger than most town markets in centuries past, with a hundred times the variety, a souk, a mall, an agora, a Fulton Street. Miles of aisles. When I was researching the article last fall, I discovered that in 1940 a grocery might stock an average of three hundred items, but now the "modern" well-stocked supermarket has on average fifty thousand different products. Spenser and Angelotti claimed seventy-five thousand. Spenser and Angelotti had a large wine shop. A flower shop with a giant parasol and bunches of flowers in tin buckets like a European flower market. The take-out, called Eat and Run. A coffee bar called Coffee Café.

Now Bruno turned on all the lights in the place, maybe trying to drive away ghosts himself. The store occupied an entire block, if you counted the parking lot, and the building itself was huge. An average supermarket is twenty-five thousand to thirty-five thousand square feet. This store was forty-five thousand. Two-thirds of it was sales space, the public part. Of this the west wall was made of glass windows and glass front doors. There was a gigantic round window set high into the north wall of the store. Bruno Angelotti had told me that most supermarkets have as few windows as possible, in order to use the walls for sales shelves. He said he didn't want a store that felt like a prison, hence the round window. It was about twenty feet across and reinforced by metal strips in latitude and longitude lines, like a globe. In the center was a pale blue glass silhouette of North and South America. The implication was that Spenser and Angelotti brought foods from all over the world to their Chicago customers. The south wall of the store had a very tall, narrow window with an arched top. It reached almost to the high ceiling, thirty feet up. It dominated the view in that direction and made you feel that the store was open to the sky. You could always see clouds or sunlight through it in the daytime. But it was narrow, leaving most of the south wall free to be used for sales space. The east wall of the marketing floor was actually an interior divider that backed up to a hall giving access to the behind-the-scenes offices and workrooms.

To my right, the fruit market stretched away, a confetti of colors. The yellow grapefruit were so packed with juice that the skins looked as shiny and tight as balloons. The Clementine tangerines nestled like flattened oranges, coy, with their dimple up, their skins a bright cadmium orange. There were pale yellow Anjou pears. Granny Smith apples, spring-grass green. Arching over the fruit display was a long red-and-white-striped awning, reminiscent of an outdoor farmers' market in Tuscany.

Somebody said, "Cat?" I turned away reluctantly from the beauty of the fruit department to the meat department. I walked to a cold case and stood looking in.

"Show us where you got the bone, Cat," McCoo said.

"Right about here." I pointed to a section just past the beef patties, where there were plastic-wrapped packages of suet and trays of soup bones. "Right there, I think."

McCoo said to the detectives, "Well, get started."

They and the evidence techs blinked a bit. McCoo said, "Empty the case. Take anything that was packaged in this store. Not those, for instance." He pointed at several commercially packaged brands of lard nearby. "No cured meat, like ham or corned beef, no poultry, no fish."

It was extremely unusual for the chief of detectives to go out on any case. In fact, I knew that being taken out of investigations was one of the things McCoo disliked about his repeated promotions. Every advance in rank moved him farther away from field work.

"Don't *any*body walk into the butcher area," he said.

Maybe it was just as well that Sam had to go home and sleep. Bruno Angelotti needed a friend. Spenser was his partner and his friend, too, I supposed, but Spenser was too freaked out by the assault on the bottom line to be cuddly and warm right now. I put an arm around Bruno.

And isn't that the most annoying thing about behaving responsibly? So often it turns out that you did the right thing. And if so, how could you even have entertained the idea of doing the irresponsible thing? I was glad I was here because Bruno was starting to look sick.

One of the detectives picked up a neatly

labeled package of ground pork as an example of what to take to the lab and, gesturing with it, said to the techs, "Call for a second wagon. You'll need to take all of this chopped stuff."

Spenser stood back, aghast.

I watched as Spenser and Angelotti realized viscerally what their minds had recoiled from back at the ME's office. If part of the leg bone of an adult human being had been in the meat case, exactly where was the rest of him?

Bruno Angelotti turned fish-belly pale and bolted for the men's room. Henry Spenser watched him go. Barkley the lawyer suddenly put his hand over his mouth and ran gagging after Bruno to the men's room.

Spenser wrapped both arms around himself and gazed at the floor.

The meat would have to go through the hall and then out the back doors into the waiting evidence van. The access hall extended the whole width of the store behind the public part. Doors led off it into several offices, work and storage areas, and from each of the work and storage areas outside loading doors could be opened to the back delivery alley. One of the biggest work areas was the bakery. The two evidence techs and the two detectives had pushed a few three-shelved steel carts on wheels from the bakery through the hall into the meat sales area. They propped open the double doors to the bakery and the double doors from the hall to the sales floor.

The techs loaded packages onto the carts. Lots of packages. Ground beef, ground lamb, ground pork, roasts, steaks, stew meat, chops, bones, and suet.

"Take all that out through the rear bakery doors," McCoo said. "Not the butcher shop."

They trekked meat to the evidence van while we stood in the store and watched and made occasional self-conscious remarks about the weather. After several trips, the meat cases were denuded of 80 percent of the beef, lamb, pork, and veal.

Of course, while this meat might be evidence, we all knew that the butcher shop was ground zero.

When the meat cases were emptied, McCoo walked slowly into the hall and over to the butcher shop doors to peer in. We trailed after him. Like the deli/catering kitchen and the bakery, the butcher shop had double hall doors with porthole windows, so that during busy workdays you could tell whether somebody else was coming out toward you as you were charging through in the other direction. They weren't large enough to see much else, and McCoo propped the doors open.

The butcher shop looked somewhat like a large operating room. Shining handsaws, power saws in their own floor stands, stainless steel tables. Large meat grinders, with big hoppers, mixers, sausage grinders, sausage stuffers with their snoutlike ends. There were rolling conveyor belts that carried meat in white polystyrene trays through a shrink-wrapping and labeling machine. None of this was in operation tonight, of course. There were no butchers here now.

There was not a fleck of meat on the tables or floor. No meat had been left out around the room. Three stainless steel doors in the far wall probably led into refrigerators; the doors were so clean they mirrored the room.

The place was spotless. Dr. Thelonius Morgan from the health department was standing in the hall with us, also peering in the doors. He said, "Not bad!"

But McCoo wasn't pleased at all. "Spenser! You said you closed it down. You didn't say you had them wash everything."

"They clean as they go," Spenser said uneasily.

"Did you tell anybody to clean up after work ended?"

"Uh, I just—I may have said they could *finish* washing up."

McCoo and the two detectives exchanged sour glances. One of the detectives shrugged and said, "Well, we'll keep on keeping on. I don't want anybody walking around in there until the evidence techs get through."

The prescribed approach to a crime scene calls for "preserving its integrity." This means nobody, not even the senior detective on the case, gets in until the evidence techs are done processing it. In actual practice, if the superintendent of police, or the mayor, or even the area commander wants to go tromping through with both feet, nobody would have the guts to stop him. But it's not supposed to happen. And in this case, Chief of Detectives McCoo definitely knew better. He and I and both detectives, and everybody else, clumped together

24

in the hall, peering in, while the two evidence technicians entered the butcher shop.

The two techs from the crime lab, Chet Parker and Phillis Humphries, stood in the doorway wearing expressions of disbelief. Humphries, the older and more experienced ET, put her hands on her hips and muttered, "This is some kind of cruel joke."

"I wish," McCoo said.

"I know. I'm on *Candid Camera*."

"Sorry. No."

Humphries said, "You actually want us to look for *blood* in a *butcher shop*?"

"Yes," said both detectives and McCoo all together. And McCoo added, "We'll figure out which is human and which is animal later."

"Great. Just great," Humphries growled.

The fatter, older detective, whose name was Torvil, said, "People been using this place all day?"

McCoo said, "Yup. My best guess, the crime took place twenty hours ago. And the space has been in constant use since then. We'll deal with it. Before anybody else gets in there, Humphries, you take the one-to-one Polaroid. I want photos of all the footprints visible to the naked eye."

She picked the camera out of her bag, which she left in the doorway, and entered the large work area. The thinner detective said, "But, boss, people must've tracked all over everything all day."

"I know. We'll do it anyway." He was well aware this would be a case the media picked over, if the facts ever became known.

When Humphries had finished, McCoo said, "Everybody stay out in the hall. We're going to turn the lights off."

The fluorescents went out, and although there was a distant glow from the lights in the store, here in the hall we were in deep darkness. We crowded around the double doors to watch. Humphries put on a mask, took a spray bottle from her kit, and began to spray a fine mist. Luminol.

Slowly the floor began to glow. A cool, green luminescence appeared. As she worked her way across, the floor glowed—everywhere! There was scarcely one inch that didn't have some trace of blood.

"Oh, fine!" Humphries said. "It's a floor polish *and* a blood product!"

Brighter streaks came up. These were marks made by a mop. But at several places across the room there were footprints where none had been visible before.

Humphries tagged each footprint with a numbered paper square. Then she went back with a Kodak Ektagraphic EF Visualmaker and photographed each one, making notes of each footprint's location. Last, she switched to an ordinary Polaroid camera with extra-high-speed film and took panoramic pictures of the room with the markers in place. Finally, she removed sheets of rubbery plastic, about twelve inches long. She took one sheet at a time, peeled the backing off it, and pressed the adhesive side down on a footprint. First making sure she had smoothed out all the air bubbles, she pulled the sheet up off the floor, smoothed the backing onto it again, and labeled it with an indelible marker. She repeated this process with all the footprints she had identified.

The detective hit the lights. The clump of us in the doorway sighed as one. McCoo looked at Detective Torvil's sour face and, answering his unspoken thought, said, "Yeah. I know. Probably the footprints of whoever washed the floor."

"Sure," Humphries said, "they must be, because you can tell to look at them they were made wet."

"You can *never* be sure," McCoo said. "Suppose the guy who cleaned up washed the middle of the floor"—he waved his arm—"from the back door to the hall door, and around the tables, and missed all the corners and didn't bother to do the places that looked clean. Suppose the killer left a shoe print under the sink?"

Detective Torvil grudgingly said, "That's possible."

"So keep working," McCoo said to the techs.

McCoo and the detectives remained in the hall.

"Sure, let's do it." Humphries opened another kit.

Evidence techs have a pattern of evidence gathering. But they also take suggestions, not always cheerfully, from the detectives, who get ideas of what might have happened at the crime scene and how far to go with the search. In this case, the chief of detectives was looming over the detectives. This made them antsy.

They started to point out what they wanted done.

"Bag the towels," Detective Torvil said.

"And take samples behind the tables," the younger detective said.

Humphries muttered, "We know that."

"Print the paper towel dispenser."

"We know that, too."

"And the dishwasher handle."

"Yes, dammit."

"And underneath the handle."

Humphries said, "Hey, Torvil! There's a meat hook around here someplace with your name on it."

Torvil shut up.

Chet Parker brushed black fingerprint powder on the white front of the heavy-duty industrial dishwasher. He used a soft, rounded nylon brush, which he dipped briefly into the powder; then he flicked the brush handle with his finger, shaking off excess powder. With curving strokes, he brought out the friction ridges, or fingerprints, dark against the silvery stainless steel.

He opened a roll of fingerprint tape. This is cellophane tape, very much like ordinary Scotch tape. The roll was two inches wide. He smoothed a chunk of it over each fingerprint he developed, taking care to eliminate air bubbles, as Humphries had done with the foot-prints. He pressed the lifters against one print, then another, noting where each print had been found.

Meanwhile, Humphries was working on the implements, the knives, spatulas, saws, larding needles, scoops, spoons, scrapers, hammers, and tenderizing mallets. It was a daunting job. She used a roll of fingerprint tape like Chet Parker's. But she was working with a lot of curved surfaces, mostly the handles of tools, and I noticed that with those she switched to a rubbery lifter that came in single, small sheets.

Parker said, "I think I'll Superglue the glass stuff, sir."

McCoo said, "Sure. But not the metal things."

"Okay."

Cyanoacrylate fuming was developed by the Japanese National Police in the late 1970s. A while back, the cops actually used Superglue, but now they use one of its ingredients, a cyanoacrylate methyl ester product sold for police use. It brings up latent prints well, especially on things like glass or plastic bags. But Superglue fuming can mess up biological material. If they want to test the fingerprint for human blood, they won't use fuming. So apparently a decision had now been made to retain the ability to find out whether a person with human blood on his hands had handled the tools, and, if so, which tools.

Chet packed the small number of drinking glasses and glass measuring cups into a box.

Detective Torvil turned to Henry Spenser and said, "We have to take the saws and saw blades with us."

Henry said, "Why?"

"That bone was cut. We need to identify the blade that cut it."

"Just exactly how do you think we're going to run a business here without meat saws?"

"Maybe you can borrow some?"

"Shit!"

"We'll get these back as soon as we can, sir."

Spenser sighed. Chet took the blades out of the table saw and the band saw.

Humphries used a Polaroid CU-5 to photograph several fingerprints in situ. This camera has a ring light attachment and "barn doors" that show the photographer how big the visual field is. It's used only for extreme close-ups.

Half an hour went by.

Humphries brought out a gadget that emitted a narrow red beam of laser light. I have a friend who uses a small one of these when he lines up shots playing pool, but originally these were surveyors' tools. Humphries set it one foot in from the north wall. Then, while Chet held a ruler for her, she went along taking swabs of the floor at one-foot intervals. Each swab was a tiny square of gauze dipped in sterile water; it was then rubbed on the floor and dropped into a paper envelope, which she numbered.

When she reached the end of the light beam, she and Chet moved it one foot farther from the wall and worked down it again in one-foot intervals.

This could take all night.

McCoo said to Spenser, "While we have a little time, Mr. Spenser, tell me what hours the butcher shop is unoccupied."

"About midnight to five A.M., allowing for the cleaners."

"Always?"

"Yes. A lot of supermarkets have butchers in at night to grind hamburger and cut steak and so on for the next day. We're not set up quite the usual way. We have two eight-hour shifts of butchers. There's a reason for this. We do many, many more specialty cuts than most stores. More than any other store I know of, in fact. We like to think that if somebody walks into Spenser and Angelotti at three o'clock in the afternoon and wants a rack of lamb or a crown roast of pork or whatever, we can have it ready for them before they've finished their other shopping. We even get suckling pig in for our customers, although that takes a day's notice."

This was turning into an ad for Spenser and Angelotti. McCoo said, "Go on, please."

"So, my point is, we have senior, skilled master meat cutters on duty all day. Two shifts. Seven A.M. to three, and three to eleven P.M. The second shift does two hours of prep work after the store closes at nine, or ten on Saturday. And then the morning staff of butchers gets here at seven A.M. to start fresh ground beef and so on for the day. This kind of schedule also allows for the place to close down for a thorough cleaning every evening." He stopped abruptly, realizing that McCoo wasn't pleased about the thorough cleaning that had happened this particular evening.

I thought to myself that a graveyard shift of butchers might also be more costly than day shifts, a fact that would interest Spenser with his bottom-line thinking. But then, heck, I'm a cynic.

McCoo said, "So the store is empty from when? Eleven P.M.?"

"Usually from midnight, after the cleaners get done. Bruno and I sometimes work late, too. And we do a lot of catering, you know, and the catering staff sometimes—rarely—gets back here from an event as late as two A.M. Then they have to put stuff away and load their soiled equipment into their dishwashers. Into the deli/catering dishwashers, not the butcher shop ones."

"So they would be out by . . . ?"

"One A.M. usually, I would think. But last night, twelve."

"And the staff arrives at seven A.M.?"

"The butchers do. The bakery staff gets here at five A.M. A lot of the bakery equipment is automated, so the dough's either started automatically or it's waiting in 'closets' at various temperatures. Most of it needs a second rising in pans. And the bakers have to start the ovens."

"I'll need to get a schedule for last night specifically. So ordinarily the store is not staffed between one A.M. and five A.M. What about night watchmen?"

"Night watchmen are going the way of the dodo, Chief McCoo. We have an alarm system. We got rid of our last watchman when we found him asleep in the wine shop in the morning surrounded by three empty Sauterne bottles, the bones of a barbecued chicken, and an empty half-gallon container of rocky road ice cream. Poor man didn't even know Sauterne doesn't go with barbecued chicken."

After Chet Parker and Phillis Humphries finished the floor swabs, Chet ran a Dustbuster, changing its special paper bags frequently and marking which bag had been used where. Bruno had come out of the bathroom, pale, sad, with wet hair, and was pacing in the hall. Henry Spenser pounded one hand into the palm of the other.

Humphries now cast a raking light from a flashlight against the butcher shop walls. She used white light, then red, then green, hoping to bring up stains that had been mostly wiped off. Mumbling, "You might as well have wallpapered it with blood," she wiped areas, bagged, labeled, wiped, bagged, labeled. Finally she turned to McCoo and said, "I don't do windows."

He laughed. "You're lucky there aren't any. Because if there were, you would."

Chet opened the drain traps in the sinks. With a ladle he drew out the water and the yucky crud in it, bottled and tagged it. Of four sinks, two had garbage disposals. Above them was a sign: HEALTH REGULATIONS FORBID THE DISPOSAL OF SIGNIFICANT AMOUNTS OF MEAT WASTE. USE SINKS ONLY FOR ORDINARY WASHING PROCEDURES. Chet swabbed the disposals inside thoroughly with gauze squares. Then he unscrewed the hex nut at the bottom of the U-bends and drained everything inside, which was a disgusting black glop, into bottles. He capped and labeled the bottles. Last, he ran a plumber's snake, a hooked wire, down the sink through the drains, hooking or pushing out any solid bits. I watched for human hair, but I didn't see any.

Humphries used forceps and small squares of white cloth moistened with sterile distilled water to rub anything that looked like a stain. These she placed in unstoppered test tubes, labeling each as she collected it. They always let biological evidence dry. If it stays wet, it will degrade. A very few stains were thicker streaks. These she scraped with a knife onto squares of white paper, which she folded, labeled, and placed in paper envelopes, which she also labeled. They never use plastic bags for biological evidence, for the same reason. They don't want it to stay moist. Once in a while they will collect liquid blood in a test tube of saline, but you have to get it to the crime lab within twenty-four hours, and we didn't have any liquid blood here anyway.

Chet and Phillis announced that we could now walk on the floor.

McCoo got a key from Spenser, entered the butcher shop, and unlocked one of the walk-in refrigerator doors. The light inside went on automatically. Sides of beef hung on hooks. Opposite them stainless steel shelves held a bewildering array of packages, some plastic, some aluminum foil, some refrigerator paper.

"Well, there you go," he said. "Remove anything that could be human."

I was pleased to see that Mr. Barkley, the lawyer, had not yet emerged from the men's room. He'd been gone a long time.

Spenser said, "Surely you know you don't need to take sides of beef. They're obviously—what they are. Cows."

He unwrapped a foil package. "And this is corned beef. Branded by the manufacturer," Spenser said.

Bruno Angelotti pulled me away.

"Cat, I would like to ask you something," he said, with his slight accent.

"Go ahead."

"Henry thinks the worst is over," Bruno said. "He will keep this quiet if he can, get the insurance to cover, and all that."

"Yes. Keep the business running."

"Of course, of course. Our lovely store. We make good food, Cat, you know that. Wonderful food. Pure, safe food."

"I *do* know that."

"There's something he doesn't realize yet. He sees, and I see, what may have happened here. May not have. But it may. What he hasn't thought about is this: If a man was killed here, was it one of us?"

"Us?"

"My family of employees. My wonderful managers and cooks and salespeople. Was it one of my Spenser and Angelotti family who was killed?"

"Or—maybe one of you is the murderer?"

"Oh! Oh, my God! That would be a catastrophe."

"You have to be prepared."

"You see? All the worse. And Chief McCoo, who is your friend, is nevertheless a policeman and will suspect us. Of course he will. We knew what was here, what the meat department looked like, how it worked, how you could cut up a body, you see."

"Yes, I know, Mr. Angelotti."

"And soon we will all suspect each other and no one will know what the police are thinking."

"That's true."

"So, Cat, what I want is this. Will you come and work here, starting in the morning? Please. I will pay you. You will be a—a deli assistant, or ad copywriter, or catering consultant, or whatever you want."

"But Mr. Angelotti, you're right—Harold McCoo is my friend. And if I hear anything that actually points to a killer, I'll have to tell him. Won't that be like having a police spy in the store?"

He smiled. "Call me Bruno. No, it will be more like having a police liaison. You have to understand, I have not killed anybody. I am afraid that if time goes by without a solution someone will leak to the media the information about what happened here. This wonderful emporium is my life. Will you work here, and pretend you don't know me or Henry? And listen to what people are saying?"

✧ 4 ✧

"Tie the veal shin meat to the bones so
that it will not fall off during cooking."

McCoo said, "I don't like you working there."

"Oh, don't be such a stick-in-the-mud." I
was sitting in the hard visitor's chair in his
office first thing the next morning, Sunday.
McCoo's own chair is a leather-upholstered
affair with padded arms. It sits on big, silent,
well-oiled casters. Except for his coffeemaker,
new espresso machine, and tiny refrigerator, it's the only luxurious furnishing in
his office. His desk is functional metal; the
bookcases and files are metal; and he inten-
tionally has no rug. He likes to zip around in
his chair from desk to file cabinet to coffeemaker to bookcase.

The new La Pavoni machine was up to
pressure and the air was filled with a rich
aroma. McCoo had ground the beans fresh
when I entered his office and funneled distilled water into the tank. In his tiny refrigerator he kept real cream.

A true gentleman, McCoo. No matter how
much he might disagree with me, he was
always the perfect host. "Something new I'm
trying," he said. He blasted steam through the
beans. "A Vietnamese coffee. Rich and robust

37

without quite the bitterness of the Honduran I tried last week."

"Smells great." I needed the coffee badly. I had brought in the lasagna I'd been so proud of, made with Spenser and Angelotti's ground beef. It gave me shivers to look at it, and it now sat congealed on McCoo's desk, waiting to go to the lab. He ignored it.

"I am not going to say one word to encourage you," he went on. "You're not a cop, and not even a city employee. If I so much as breathe 'okay' and you get killed, your heirs could sue the city."

"I don't have any heirs."

"If there's a few million dollars in the offing, you'll develop heirs you never knew you had."

"True. McCoo, all I'm asking is a little help. I feel so awfully sorry for Bruno. He loves that store. He loves the food he creates. I saw him make a *Vacherin* with the pastry chef once, and I can tell you he piped the meringue around the center with more gentle affection than most people show their human lovers."

"Yeah, well, that's gonna be a big help if you're attacked with a filleting knife."

"I won't be attacked."

"It's happened before. You can't walk your bird without being attacked."

"I have to help him, McCoo. With or without your support. I don't need your permission."

I got up and stomped huffily around the room while McCoo said, "You're being egotistical. I have four experienced detectives on the case and they're perfectly able to find the killer."

"I can get inside information. Nobody will know I'm reporting to you."

"No."

I glanced at the bag of coffee beans.

"And, McCoo, I would think you *especially* would want to do all you could to help Bruno Angelotti."

"Why?"

I held up the red-and-white-check-patterned bag. "Where did you find this wonderful, new Vietnamese specialty coffee, McCoo?"

The price tag was headed in flowing letters: "From the Coffee Market of Spenser and Angelotti."

✧ 5 ✧

"Chop carrots, onions, celery, and garlic. This mixture, before cooking, is called a *battuto*. Sauté in melted butter in a heavy casserole until the onions are transparent and the mass turns into a lightly browned *soffrito*."

The immense parking lot was studded with ornate light posts, wrought-iron in appearance although in fact probably aluminum. Each post held two acorn-shaped cream glass lights at the top, at the end of curved arms. On each post was a letter and number to help you remember where you parked. I was in D9. Spenser and Angelotti knew their Chicago. Without the lot, street parking around here would take longer to find than it took to make *cassata alla Siciliana* from scratch. Parking in a commercial garage cost more per hour than I make working.

From the arms of many of the light stanchions hung red-and-white-check-bordered banners with advertising. The D9 one said JUST ARRIVED—CHILEAN POMPANO FILLETS. A man on a stepladder two rows away unhooked a banner: STRIP SIRLOIN—AGED TO PERFECTION. As I watched, he raised a replacement banner that read IN OUR DELI—SIX WAYS TO USE COUSCOUS.

The entry doors of Spenser and Angelotti were recessed under a kind of verandahlike arcade roof, which was why I didn't see the picketers until I walked right into them.

A dozen slender creatures formed a church choir–style grouping next to the main doors. There were six ethereal men and six ethereal women, and, swear to God, they looked like angels. They were dressed all in white, milk white, pale cream, and eggshell, the men mostly in natural unbleached crushed cotton shirts with cotton pants, and the women in looser-fit pants or filmy skirts, with loose floating tunics or wide-sleeve shirts.

They were slender to the point of etiolated medieval church sculptures, with long thin hands and faces. Their hair hung clean but lank and long. Their hands were bony.

Three held large photographs between long, bony fingers. The photos showed chickens in cages, calves in cages, cows being injected with something, presumably hormones. Two of the picketers held signs: EATING MEAT IS MURDER. And MUST YOU KILL?

Very softly, they sang songs of love.

I stopped to stare. The young woman nearest me said, "Think what you do when you buy meat. Picture the death you cause."

"All right," I said. "That's fair enough. To ask a person to think."

"Because you don't see it, you put it out of your mind."

"That's true."

She said, "A vegetarian diet is perfectly healthful. We don't have to cause death to be healthy."

"I can't promise I'll reform, but I do take you seriously. You have a consistent and kindly point of view."

She smiled beatifically and several of the others chorused, "Thank you."

Heading into the store, I knew I was going to feel terrible if I left at the end of my day here with a plump chicken for roasting.

On my way through the store to Bruno Angelotti's office, I passed a table laden with various bottles of olive oil, some veggies, and an electric frying pan. A dozen chairs were set up in two rows facing the table. A woman dressed in a navy skirt, white shirt, and a red-and-white-checked chef's apron dropped a battered mushroom into oil, where it and its fellows sizzled temptingly. A dozen people

41

stood or sat watching. She was Spenser and Angelotti's food educator.

"I know you've heard that you shouldn't fry or sauté in olive oil," she said, in a sweet but extremely competent voice. "That isn't true. The important thing is not to exceed 350 degrees. Do *not* heat the oil until smoke forms over it, no matter what you may have read. Overheated olive oil turns bitter."

When I reached Bruno's office, I said, "Did you see those picketers?" Bruno and Henry Spenser had tiny offices right next to each other at the north end of the interior hall, and Henry was standing in Bruno's, punching his right hand impatiently into the palm of his left.

"Yeah, we saw them," Henry said. "Damned Fern Ffolke!"

"Why are they singling you out?"

Henry said, "They're not singling us out. They're picketing a lot of places. All in the Loop or near Loop, though. Places where they'll get media coverage."

Bruno said, "They held a vigil last week at the site where the old Chicago stockyards used to be."

"For an ethereal bunch," I said, "they sound media sophisticated."

"Very," Henry said grimly.

I said, "Well, I guess you have to be these days."

Bruno said in a tone of deep pity, "They hardly eat anything. Only enough to stay alive."

"I have doubts about this business of hiring

you," Henry Spenser said, echoing McCoo. "But I've agreed to go along with Bruno. The police have been nothing but trouble. And expense. Fifteen hundred pounds of meat went out of here last night."

"Better safe than sorry."

"Oh, really?" Henry snarled. "They were here until five A.M. They took away all the garbage that was left in the butcher shop. Fingerprinted the whole place. We had black powder residue all over the stainless steel."

"Certainly you want them to be thorough."

He snorted. "I had to call two of our cleaners in early at time-and-a-half to get the place back in shape before the butchers came to work."

"That's too bad."

"And now, with the recall announcements we've had to set up a whole damn desk and two staffers to take in the meat that people are returning. Plus a lot of them want cash, not food credit. How can you blame them? We've told them there was contamination caused by possible sabotage here, so why should they want to buy something *else* that could be contaminated? Meanwhile, the meat cases are half empty. We're losing a fortune! God only knows what this will do to our business long-term."

Personally, I thought he was extremely fortunate the mayor didn't want the real reason talked about. I also thought he'd be very lucky if there was no leak. But I didn't say that.

"And announcements on television and

43

radio and in the newspapers!" Bruno Angelotti said. "It's so embarrassing!"

"Horribly embarrassing!" Spenser said.

"Shaming."

"Terrible!"

This was the first time I had heard these two men, so different in personality, sound absolutely identical. And really, I felt sorry for both of them, even though I liked Bruno more. It took years of hard work to build a business like theirs. Probably years of risk at the beginning.

I said mildly, "People have very short memories. They'll forget in a week or so that there was ever a problem, and business will come back."

Bruno said, "While we worry about our losses, we must remember that someone has died."

He was so right.

They had supplied an announcement to the media. The same text had been printed on large signs, maybe four feet by six feet, and set on display easels just inside each door, plus a smaller one in the meat department.

The signs read: WE REGRET THAT A POSSI-BILITY OF CONTAMINATION FORCES US TO RECALL ALL BEEF, PORK, LAMB, AND VEAL PRODUCTS, AS WELL AS BEEF BONES SOLD ON FRIDAY, APRIL 2 AND SATURDAY, APRIL 3. PLEASE BRING SUCH PRODUCTS TO THE STORE AND WE WILL REFUND FIVE TIMES THE SELLING PRICE OR PROVIDE AN EQUIVALENT AMOUNT OF MERCHANDISE. THE CONTAMINANT IS CON-SIDERED NONINJURIOUS AND WAS NOT CAUSED

BY THE STORE, BUT THE PRODUCT NEVER-
THELESS SHOULD NOT BE CONSUMED.

"Did your lawyer, Mr. Barkley, word that announcement?"

Bruno said, "No. Uh—"

"What?"

"He has gone to the hospital."

"Is he sick?"

"Uh—it seems to be a sort of nervous breakdown."

"Oh."

Changing the subject, Bruno said, "Perhaps you'd better pretend not to know Henry and me very well. The staff will talk more freely to you if they don't think you're some sort of spy."

When I wrote the article, I dealt mostly with the two men about their aspirations that led to the founding of the store. Fortunately, I hadn't met any of the regular staff.

"I suppose you're determined to be here," Henry said.

"Henry!" Bruno said. Then to me, "I think it is best for you to be a catering consultant. As a cashier you would have very little chance to roam the store and talk with people. To write ad copy you wouldn't even need to be in the store. And you cannot be a cook or chef, because you need health department and union papers to work directly with food."

"I see. What will I do?"

"You can answer phone requests for catering. If you're in catering, you will have reason to go to various departments in the store to see what is in stock. Therefore, you can talk to

45

people. You may pretend to want to see what's especially good, because you will want to include it on a menu for an event. You understand?"

"Perfectly."

"And this will be believable to the staff because our catering manager is on vacation."

"How will I know what I'm doing?"

"Oh, Paul-Michel Cartier, our assistant catering manager, is in charge. You won't have to actually *know* anything."

"Mmm. That's nice."

"And, of course, as I discovered when you wrote about us, you do know food."

"As an enthusiast, not as an expert. Like I'm not a linguist, but I can order food in twenty languages."

"In fact, since Serge Gretzka is not here, you will be a genuine help to us."

"Oh? Gretzka's the catering manager? When did he leave?"

"Friday night. After work."

"He left *Friday night*?"

"Do you know where this Serge Gretzka was going?"

"Yes. Panama City, Florida," Bruno said. "He sublets a small condo from some people for two weeks every year. He's a golfer, and he said that was a good place to golf. I don't understand golf myself."

I had spent two hours with Paul-Michel, the assistant catering manager. Fortunately,

Spenser and Angelotti had large forms on which you entered the details about the event a customer wanted catered. And when I say details, I mean details. It wasn't simply: Write down the time, place, nature of the celebration, number of guests, price, and then we send food. There was an entire page just for beverages, and another page giving a choice of wines and *timing* of the wines. Which ones were to be served with the appetizers, which with each course, and so on. A whole page for dessert wines and brandies. There were questions about any known allergies of any of the guests. There were detailed questions about religious preferences and taboos and half a sheet telling what sort of foods *never to suggest* to which ethnic groups. There were specific orders about what sorts of foods *may not* be served during buffets to people standing up. Apparently nobody was going to dribble barbecue sauce on their shirts at a Spenser and Angelotti function.

And that was just the hard copy. All this information also had to be entered into the computer.

In addition, there were five three-ring binders of recipes and Bruno's *Notes on Food: Specialties of the Spenser and Angelotti Cuisine*, which we catering experts were supposed to use to suggest interesting possibilities to the customers. In case our imagination flagged, there was one three-ring binder that held a hundred and fifty suggested full menus, some general and some categorized by event— wedding, baby shower, birthday (subdivided into infant, young boy, young girl, teen, sweet sixteen, adult, elderly), football party, bridge party, twenty-fifth wedding anniversary, fiftieth anniversary, funeral, and dozens more.

I had sneaked into Bruno Angelotti's office during my break. He was drinking Colombian coffee with just a dash of amaretto and offered me some. Naturally I seized it instantly.

"This is almost like visiting McCoo," I said.

"Why is that?"

"You want to butter up McCoo, get him talking about coffee."

Bruno smiled, the first smile I'd seen on him since the awful events of last night. He loved people who loved food.

"This was Gretzka's regularly scheduled vacation?" I asked.

"Yes, in a way. It has been scheduled for some time. However, it is not the time of year he usually takes it."

"What do you mean?"

"Ordinarily, his vacation is later. In October. He says October in Florida is good for golf. But he's been feeling tired. So he moved it up."

"Moved it up recently?"

"Oh, no. Several weeks ago."

"So can you call this Gretzka at his condo in Panama City?"

"I suppose. He should have left the information in his file."

"Please. Do it."

"Call him? What do you want to know?"

"I want to know if he ever got there."

Bruno's mouth opened into a big O. He put the coffee cup down on the desk and raised both hands to the sides of his head.

✦ 6 ✦

"Heat olive oil in a heavy skillet, but do not let it burn."

"I'm the new catering assistant. I'm helping the catering manager, Mr. Cartier, while Mr. Gretzka is on vacation."

The assistant butcher said, "Well, you've certainly picked the worst possible time to get hired."

Buddy Dack looked so much like a cartoon pig, it made me nervous that I might say something insensitive about pork. He was plump and pink, with cheeks so smooth they looked as if they would never need a shave, a flat nose pushed back into his face, tiny little ears that didn't quite come to points, and shiny skin on his face that went all the way back over his bald head. His body was rounded, and his feet and hands were tiny.

How dare he cut and trim pork? I wondered.

Bruno Angelotti had warned me not to call him a butcher. "They are 'meat-cutting technicians' now," he said.

49

"Why is this a bad time?" I asked.

"Bad time for you. Everything's in a mess."

"Why is that?"

"Oh, some stupid *contamination* thing. We were told by the health department to resterilize everything this morning! They say it isn't dangerous. If it isn't dangerous, why recall the products?" Two assistant butchers stopped to listen.

"Well, maybe it's unpleasant." I phrased it that way, wondering if he knew anything more than he was letting on.

But he said, "If something tastes unpleasant, the customer will bring it back so fast it will make your head spin."

"But you wouldn't want your customers to have a bad experience with your meat if you could avoid it, would you?"

"Oh, I suppose not. Anyway, what are you in here for?"

"To find out what's available. I'm told a lot of meat was removed. We need to know what we can use. We have two catering jobs tonight and one tomorrow."

"Well, I can tell you it's been just about impossible! Try to get deliveries on a Sunday! How do they expect me to do my job?"

"I don't know, Mr. Dack. What do you have?"

"They left me the cured meats. The ones in their original packaging. Corned beef. Hams. They left me the whole sides of beef, and the pork roasts and shoulders. Some rib roasts."

Anything clearly identifiable as nonhuman,

in other words. "Mr. Dack, don't you wonder what the contaminant was?"

"I haven't got time to wonder, girl! Tell me what you need, and I'll see if we've got it. And then leave me alone. I've got work to do."

"Can you get me four crown roasts of lamb?"

"Yeah, yeah. I can do crown roast. They left me the lamb quarters."

"And I need two really dramatically large roasts of beef, at least ten pounds each. Can you do that? You say you have sides of beef?"

"Yeah. I guess they could tell the sides weren't contaminated."

Something like that.

He went on, "But I need to replenish the sales cases. Not that I can, really, until tomorrow. But I can try."

"The catering takes precedence. These people have ordered and sent in their down payment. They have guests coming tonight—"

"Yeah, yeah, yeah. Okay."

"Other than that, I think we can make do with chicken. And duck."

"Yeah, yeah."

"Then, if it's okay with you, I'll walk around here and see if I can come up with any ideas."

"Well, don't get in the way. All we need is, you fall into the meat grinder and get turned into sausage."

He *had* to be innocent of the murder. Nobody would make a remark like that who knew there'd been human parts in the meat case.

✧   ✧   ✧

Dack stood at a stainless steel table, trimming extra fat away from the long strip of lamb ribs, his knife flashing, bending the strip into a crown, the ribs curving up and out, with the center open for stuffing. He whipped string around the crown and, using some gadget that pulled the string tight, tied it in less time than it takes to tell about it. Then he did three more.

On his left hand he wore a steel-mesh glove to prevent cuts. I had seen similar gloves worn by autopsy surgeons over their latex gloves when the cadaver was suspected of a communicable disease.

Meat cutting is a craft and an art and requires lots of intense training. I don't think I could do it without weeks of instruction, and I know I couldn't do it anywhere nearly as fast.

But I could easily have done the meat *packaging* at Spenser and Angelotti.

I watched another butcher trimming flank steak. Whip! Whip! Whip! The fat and gristle just fell away. Then he put the steaks through the packager. Everything was automated, once you had produced the properly cut and trimmed piece of meat. You placed the cut of meat in a white polystyrene tray. Then you went to your keyboard. The monitor presented a menu of choices—various types of meat products. You might click on "lamb shanks" or "London broil" or "boned chicken breasts" or "beef bones." When you had clicked on the type of meat, the tray automatically moved down a conveyor belt of rollers, over a digital weighing device, and onto the wrapping machine. Plastic wrap went under the tray, then up over the top, and down again on the other side to seal the package. Then heat was briefly blasted at it to shrink the wrap. As it emerged from the plastic wrapper, a small computer-controlled self-adhesive-label generator was ready with the name of the product, today's date, last date for sale, the weight, the price per pound, and the total price. Then the finished package was disgorged onto a wheeled steel cart, to be taken to a refrigerator or to the meat sales cases out in the store's selling floor.

Something teased my mind. It would have been so easy to package a bone, and so much harder to chop meat. Right then I bet myself that no human contaminant would be found in the meat sold.

Dack came over with yet another wheeled stainless steel cart. On it were the crown roasts of lamb and the two big beef roasts. "Get the chicken and duck from the store cases," he said.

"This is very efficient," I told him, gesturing at the packager.

"Yeah, yeah." He saw it every day. The novelty had long since worn off.

"Can you change the prices from here? Like can you tell it to charge five dollars a pound for ground beef?"

"Nope. It's all programmed from the office. Probably figure we'd screw it up or steal. Huh!"

"Oh. What if some food comes in that's special? That's not on the preprogrammed menu?"

"Like lark's tongues?" he asked, snickering. I assumed he was making a butcher joke.

"Right."

"If it comes in, it's put on the menu. From the office."

"Can you change the date?"

"Nope. That's either the automatic management program or it's set from the office. Don't know which. Don't care."

"Hmm. Fascinating."

I wheeled the cart into the hallway leading to the deli/catering kitchens. I thought I had been pretty slick with my questions and my casual poking around, but I looked back as the door swung closed, and he was staring after me.

The olive oil lady was still on duty after I delivered the meat to the deli/catering kitchen. She had looped back to what I assumed was the introductory part of her program. At least fifteen people now crowded around, five standing and ten or twelve sitting in the folding chairs.

"There are as many kinds of olive oil as there are kinds of food. For instance, delicate-flavored olive oils come from northwestern Italy, especially the Ligurian region." She held up a tapering glass bottle filled with beautiful angelica-green oil.

"And for more robust foods, a more robust oil, often from southern Italy, such as Apulia."

She held up a faceted flask with light golden oil.

"I can tell from your doubtful expressions that you believe the greener oils are the more robust, but you can't assume that. There are some lovely, mild, green oils where the color is derived from crushing olive leaves along with the olives themselves."

I found the Area Six detective in the storeroom. Tim Savage was interviewing employees at a wooden table in a corner. The storeroom contained all the myriad items that didn't have to be refrigerated—canned goods, packaged cereals, candy, bottled and canned juice, bottled condiments, soft drinks, and paper products—on deep racks, floor-to-ceiling height. There was a hi-lo truck for reaching the top shelves. Like the bakery and the butcher areas, this room had double loading doors leading to the outside.

Savage was a rumply, iconoclastic, easygoing man, quite unlike my semifriend, Detective Sergeant Hightower, who often undertook McCoo's more sensitive cases. Hightower was always beautifully tailored and perfectly pressed. I thought I saw McCoo's canniness here. Savage was every bit as good a detective as Sergeant Hightower, probably better because he was just as smart but didn't spend as much of his time standing on his dignity. But Savage—unlike his name—would never rile anybody up. He was really quite deceptive, because his very casualness and good nature would make the people who saw him think the whole investigation was not particularly serious, or sensitive, or secret.

You would never associate mumbly, bumbly Tim Savage with anything hush-hush. You would be wrong.

A woman wearing the Spenser and Angelotti uniform of white shirt, pressed white pants, and red-and-white-checked apron was just rising from a chair.

"I was asked to come in, Officer," I said, in a formal tone.

"Yes, ma'am," Tim said, also in a formal tone, as if he had never met me before. When the woman closed the door behind her, he chuckled. "Curiosity get the better of you, Cat?"

"You heard that McCoo said it's okay I'm here."

"Yes, but did he say you could stick your nose in everywhere?"

"Not exactly. But he knows me."

"Right. That's true. He surely knows you'll stick your nose in everywhere."

"Very funny. So what are you finding out? No, first tell me if you've been able to sell the cover story."

"Contaminant. Unpleasant but not deadly. I kind of let them think it has an unpleasant taste. And of course it was the result of sabotage. So, 'Did you see any strangers hanging around?' And, 'Where were you from Friday midnight through early morning Saturday?' And, 'Did you see anybody you know in places where they usually aren't or shouldn't be?' And, of course, the ever popular 'Did you notice anything unusual?' No problem. Also not much in the way of useful answers." He stretched, then reached behind a box and brought out a quart bottle of Simm's malt lager.

"You aren't supposed to drink on duty, are you?"

"I'm prob'ly not supposed to talk to you, either."

That was a fair point.

He added, "What're they gonna do? Fire me?"

"No. McCoo knows you're the best, or at least the most subtle." Tim had always been a bit of a rebel.

"Spare me the compliments. Besides, one is my limit."

"One compliment?"

"One beer. Plus, I skipped breakfast, and beer is full of vitamin B."

"What've you found out?"

"Found out the evidence techs are hopping mad. They have to deal with ten fifty-gallon garbage cans full of all the garbage that was collected in the store all day yesterday and last night. Plus, the ME is pissed off, too. Twenty-five-gallon and fifty-gallon drums of smelly butcher shop refuse."

"Sounds nasty."

"Is. Some of the drums contain all the trimmed-off hunks of fat from all the beef and chickens and lamb and so on. Other bins contain all the discarded bones. Some contain meat trimmings, parts that don't look good enough to sell, gristle, spoiled stuff, anything that goes past sale date."

"So assuming that the victim was killed late Friday night or very early Saturday morning, since the bones I bought Saturday were dated Saturday, they have all the relevant evidence?"

"Far as I know it's there, every disgusting scrap."

"There are very strict health department regulations," Bruno Angelotti said, his accent turning the word into "reg-a-ulations."

"Like what?" I could see he was worried. Actually, I could see he was agonized, but I couldn't help him if I didn't know anything.

"You are not allowed just to dump meat scraps or fat or any butchering by-products into the sewers. Meat refuse must all be disposed of according to elaborate health department regulations."

My mind flipped abruptly back to journalism school. J-school is very practical, but I was driven by some idealism, a notion of the old, muckraking, secret-seeking reporter, exposing evil. Ring Lardner exposing the Black Sox scandal. Sinclair Lewis, Theodore Dreiser. These guys were my heroes. I wanted to be just like them. And Upton Sinclair writing *The Jungle,* fiction based on fact and set in Chicago, laying out before the eyes of all Americans the horrors of the meatpacking industry.

Sinclair talked about "Bubbly Creek" into which the drainage of the meatpacking plants ran. It was a creek a couple of hundred feet wide, an open running sewer of waste. The grease and chemicals that drained into it mixed and worked and changed. It writhed as if huge fish were feeding in it.

Upton Sinclair changed meatpacking in Chicago.

Bruno said there were regulations on what waste you could pour in the sewers. I bet there were. I asked, "What are they?"

"Almost nothing goes into the drains. Fats are collected by recyclers. Bones are collected, scrubbed, and roasted and ground up for bonemeal fertilizer."

"And what happens to the meat scraps?"

"They are collected by a service and, I think, converted to animal feed."

"And the service doesn't come on Friday nights?"

"No. It comes Monday, Wednesday, and Friday. About ten A.M. The drums of scraps are held in the cold storage room in the butcher area between pickups."

"So Friday afternoon's and Saturday's meat scraps were in the drums the police took. What happens to the fats?"

"I am told they are rendered and—"

"And what?"

"Refined. And used in cosmetics."

Suddenly my nice Baked Coral Spice lipstick didn't seem so attractive anymore. While I was thinking this, Bruno dropped his head into his hands.

"Please tell me," I said, half afraid I knew the answer. "Is something else worrying you?"

"Serge Gretzka. He doesn't answer the phone at that condo in Panama City."

So if there were human parts in the meat refuse containers, the cops had them now. Make a mental note: Ask McCoo.

And what about Gretzka? I had asked Bruno to promise to find Tim Savage right away and tell him about the disappearance. He would pass that information on to McCoo. What was left unsaid was this: Assuming the catering manager, Gretzka, was not just delayed someplace on his way to Florida, but had vanished, was he the killer or the victim?

✧ 7 ✧

"Brown the meat and bones in the heavy skillet, turning constantly with tongs or a large spoon."

The Lake Shore Drive apartment occupied the two top floors of a high-rise in what's called the Gold Coast. It overlooked the eight lanes of Lake Shore Drive and the four lanes of the Inner Drive. We were so high up that the cars were just an interesting soundless river flowing alongside the wide expanse of Lake

Michigan to the east. At this hour of the late afternoon the sun was low over the city, and the westering light laid elongated gray-green shadows of the high-rises on the blue of the water.

Polly Cantabella was entertaining forty of her pharmaceutical CEO husband's closest friends—read "business associates, subtype: advantageous"—at an afternoon "at-home." Four P.M. to six P.M. with a lavish buffet.

The Cantabella apartment was decorated in melon shades, which, if I'm not mistaken, were trendy either the year before or the year after citrus shades. A huge cloud-soft sofa in pale ice-green honeydew, long enough to seat eight and deep enough so that people needed three starts to get up, was piled with cantaloupe pillows. The soft easy chairs were the reverse, cantaloupe with honeydew throw pillows. The area rug in the living room was the color of Santa Claus melons, ice yellow, but there were casual touches of watermelon around the room—a wide ottoman, a large Judy Chicago wall hanging made of ram's wool, and a huge colored-glass sea anemone on the ebony side table.

The dining room where we were setting up was similar, with black enamel chairs upholstered in muskmelon and a very pale cantaloupe rug. The dining room walls were vertical stripes of white and honeydew. Cocktails were being served on the balcony, with two bartenders in charge. A warm spring breeze came into the suite, laden with moisture from the lake.

The Spenser and Angelotti uniform of white with a red-and-white-checked apron didn't suit the color scheme well, and I was glad nobody had found me one to wear yet. I wore a navy suit, white shirt, and red scarf.

Polly herself had casaba-melon-colored hair and a dress of such a pale watermelon shade you almost had to see a fold of fabric from the side to realize it wasn't white.

"Come with me," she said, catching my eye.

The kitchen sported black marble floors, white bentwood chairs upholstered in bright watermelon, and white appliances, including two Sub-Zero refrigerators and a separate Sub-Zero freezer, two blenders, a bread maker, two ovens, an eight-burner cooktop, and two dishwashers. It could almost have replaced the equipment in the Spenser and Angelotti catering kitchens.

I was not the head honcho here, only the all-purpose helper. Nina Timko, one of our chefs, was in charge. Which was as it should be, since she actually knew what she was doing and I didn't. But we had been told the customer was always right, and if Polly Cantabella wanted to confide in me, I could always have Nina translate for me later on.

She took me to a quiet corner near the broiler. "Now, you just stand up for yourself," Polly said. "And don't worry about a thing."

"Yes, ma'am," I said, baffled.

"If things get difficult, you come to me."

"Yes. Ma'am."

"And just remember, I'm right behind you."

While I was still "yes, yessing," wide-eyed, she left, pausing only to cast a critical, then approving, eye over the chicken satay skewers.

I glanced at Nina, who was at the chopping block shredding lettuce. She raised her shoulders almost to her ears and let them drop. You always shred lettuce at the last minute, she had told me, or it will get limp and eventually brown. Some caterers and most salad bars used a sulphur dioxide solution to keep lettuce from turning brown. Spenser and Angelotti never, ever did.

The four crown roasts of lamb were in the ovens. Two had been all but finished at the store and were just being heated. They would be served first. The two others had been roasting here about a half hour. According to Nina, they should still be slightly pink in the center when done. Nina would carve them at the serving table. Each rib, when cut from the roast, made a lovely little lamb chop, its bone with a white paper puff on the end acting as a handle a guest could hold to eat it, although of course there were also forks.

"The superb value of the crown roast," Cartier had lectured me, "is that it is a fully satisfying meat entrée and yet acceptable finger food."

The rosemary stuffing that had baked in the center would be spooned next to it. Each crown contained about twelve or fourteen chops. This would be plenty for forty, because, along with the lamb, we were serving herbed chicken, ginger scallops, and whole cold dilled salmon. Plus three kinds of baked breads, pancetta, Genoa salad, and seven kinds of vegetables. And dessert.

"Oh, well," I said, picking up a tray of stuffed tomatoes to carry in. "Maybe Ms. Cantabella is loony."

"Don't forget the pâté," Nina said.

I found out almost immediately that Ms. Cantabella was not loony.

My main job was to make sure that all the food that was supposed to be on the table was actually on the table, and in the right sequence. I had a list. I was not considered trained enough to carve meat, or even to serve anything from the platters. But they thought I could manage to carry in new platters of food when the ones on the table started to look picked over. Nothing messy was ever allowed to remain on a Spenser and Angelotti buffet table. Every minute was opening night afresh. I was replacing a platter of polenta rounds on green leaves garnished with mushrooms when a man in a Brioni suit leaned into my face and almost made me drop the dish.

"Spenser and Angelotti?" he demanded. "Right?"

"Yes, sir." This job was ruining my naturally combative disposition.

"Gonna poison us?"

"What? I mean, no, sir."

"Had some poison in your meat products? Right?"

"No, sir. There was an unappetizing contaminant introduced into a very few items.

64

Spenser and Angelotti recalled the items immediately." I was quite pleased with myself for coming up with the word "unappetizing."

"So how do we know this is safe?"

"Even the recalled food wouldn't have hurt anybody. But this is all new."

He looked fishy-eyed at me. "Taste one."

"What?"

His face was beet red around the nose. The nose was practically in my hairline. He said, "Taste one of these."

His fat finger pointed at a satay skewer, chicken marinated in a sweet peanut sauce and cracked black pepper. Of course, we had all been instructed not to eat the food while serving. Thank goodness I didn't have to count on this as a full-time job. I picked up a skewer and nibbled the meat.

I thought about clutching my throat and falling to the floor. Rejected the idea. "Delicious," I said after finishing. And it was.

"Fine." He turned around and without another word sidled away down the buffet table, filling his plate.

He had scarcely reached the arugula when a crisply dressed woman came up to me. She was a reporter with a Chicago news channel, not an anchor, but one of the junior anchor-wanna-bes.

"You're with the caterer, aren't you?" she said sweetly.

"Yes, ma'am."

"Spenser and Angelotti?"

"Yes, ma'am."

"So what's this problem they've been having?"

I tried to scan her person for recording devices, but she was dressed in a boxy red power suit, carrying a small black patent leather purse, and even if she'd been wearing spandex, these spy gadgets are so tiny now that you might as well not try to discern them.

"Problem?" I said.

"The recall. I hear there was something terrible in their meat."

Something truly terrible *was* their meat, I thought. Maybe. "No, ma'am. As far as I know, it was harmless."

"Then why recall all that meat?"

"Well, it may have been unpleasant, but not dangerous."

"How unpleasant?"

"I don't know, ma'am."

"Did you taste it?"

"As far as I know, nobody tasted it."

"Then how did they know it was there?"

Hey, I'm a reporter, too, and I've been verbally evaded by the best of them. "Ma'am, my belief is that Spenser and Angelotti bent way over backward and recalled a lot of product that was not only safe but delicious."

Her crisp little nose wrinkled. "But how *did* they discover it? Whatever it was?"

"I believe a customer noticed a peculiarity."

The host, Karl Cantabella, also called the big CEO, cut me out of the herd as I was carrying an empty serving dish to the kitchen.

"You're the Spenser and Angelotti girl, aren't you?"

"One of them, sir."

"Don't we get a discount?"

"A discount?"

"Because of the recent unpleasantness. We went ahead and let you cater anyway. We took a risk. We ought to get a discount."

"You'd have to ask Mr. Spenser or Mr. Angelotti."

We put in four hours at the Cantabellas', having arrived at two-thirty for a 4 P.M. event. The glassware and linens people had arrived even earlier. I was exhausted and trying to help the staff rinse the serving plates when Polly Cantabella caught me.

"See now?" she said.

I smiled. Turned out that I liked her. "Yes. Amazing."

"You wondered what I was talking about, didn't you? A lot of these people live entirely on gossip. You tell Henry and Bruno not to worry. This will pass."

"I'll tell them."

"You know, they're really the best. They aren't kitschy. They're solid. They know food."

"Yes, they do."

"I mean, they don't try to force the latest 'in' food on you, like baby hamachi or hand-caught sea urchin or camel milk ice cream."

"Bruno was telling me there are a lot of inexpensive products in large, general production that are the best of their kind in the world."

"Like plain old Idaho russet potatoes for baking. There's no better anywhere. You get good solid food from Bruno. Food from around the world, special food, too, but not *just because* it's exotic. Not always cheap, but always fair. You tell him I said so."

"I will."

"And make it clear that I've told all my friends this was his food tonight and it was wonderful." She glanced briefly out the door to the hall and I saw her husband laughing with two guests. "Bruno will be feeling terrible. You be sure to explain that I'm spreading the good word."

"I will."

"Don't forget, now."

"Place the vegetables in the casserole and carefully stand the veal shanks upright on top of them."

Tonight there would be no rest for the weary. While the cleanup staff finished the Cantabella job, I went back with Nina and Frederick to Spenser and Angelotti to get the food for another event, a dinner from 7 to 9 P.M. at The

Brothers Funeral Home. The setup people were there already.

The assistant catering manager, Paul-Michel Cartier, who was a slender, carefully dressed man with a strut to his walk, had told me to be discreet and respectful when I went out on the job. Maybe he had a suspicion that I was more than just a new hire. He said, "A caterer is like a priest. He hears a lot of things, but he doesn't talk about them."

"What do you mean?"

"When you go to look at the kitchen where the dinner will be held, or check the size of the buffet table, maybe you hear the husband and wife argue. Or you arrive and the gentleman in the apartment is not the husband. Whatever. You go to Cantabellas' tonight. Mr. Cantabella is a highly placed executive, the CEO of a major pharmaceutical firm. Suppose you hear something about the company that affects the stock. Say one of their drugs has an unexpected side effect. Or one of their top execs is quitting. Suppose anything. My point is, you will never talk about it."

"I see."

"It's a question of ethics."

"Yes, I understand."

"Plus, a gossipy caterer is an out-of-work caterer."

Well, as my aunt Grace would say, "The joint was jumping." Which was an odd thing to say about a funeral home. I had arrived at six forty-five, with the cold dishes for The Brothers Funeral Home dinner.

They had closed the "home" early, having no funeral tonight and no visitations scheduled before tomorrow morning. But still it was as bizarre a scene as you'd wish. In one large room, which was ordinarily used for the display of the dearly departed, the china-and-silver people had set up eleven card-table-size tables, with four chairs at each, making places for forty-four guests. This room was still empty, except for three members of the catering staff. The noise was coming from across the hall.

The loud buzz of gaiety said clearly to me: "Cocktails in progress."

This turned out to be a large auditorium with a peaked ceiling and wooden pews. The windows were colored glass, a small rose window in front, like a generic church. Drinks were set out on a trestle table at the front, exactly the spot where you would expect to see the coffin when a funeral was in progress. The little velvet sign on a brass stand near the door, which would ordinarily hold the name of the deceased, instead read DEAD DRUNK. I mean, are these fun people or what?

Paul-Michel's orders to me that caterers are like priests and don't talk began to make real sense. Jimmie and Jerry Underhill, proprietors of The Brothers Funeral Home, would surely not wish their clients, the living ones I mean, to think this was a party place. And yet, I found out that the celebration was entirely justified. Nina said to me, "All these people are here to celebrate Jimmie's return."

"From the dead?"

"Now don't you start." Nina had a run-on way of talking that you had to work to keep up with. "It was close to that, see, because Jimmie was in a horrible automobile accident about three months ago. He was going too fast, and maybe hit a slick spot, it was January after all, although they never really found out what caused it, and he couldn't stop. Jimmie and Jerry both drive little sports cars, and he slid halfway under a truck. Pinned there for three hours. They thought he was gonna die."

"Oh." I looked over at the tall, thinnish man, now surrounded by well-wishers, who had courteously shaken my hand a few minutes ago. There was a raised white scar down the side of his forehead, ending at the right earlobe.

"He was in a coma for, I think, two weeks. He has a metal rod in one leg, and a plate in his head."

"Oh. I'm sorry. I shouldn't have been so flip."

"Can't blame you. *They* are. He's been in rehab ever since. He comes back to work tomorrow morning for the first time since the accident."

"How do you know all this?"

"Oh, Gretzka told me."

"Aren't we supposed to be like priests and not talk about the customers?"

"That's with outsiders. We always talk among *ourselves.*"

The other Underhill brother, Jerry, now

climbed onto a pew. There was a very loud general cheer. I said, "Listen to that."

"Well, they're all brothers in blood so to speak," Nina said. "Or whatever."

"This is a great day!" Jerry said. "To Jimmie!"

The gang raised glasses and sloshed drinks and yelled. One man cried, "To the resurrection of our brother, Jimmie Underhill!"

"I'm not going to climb up there with Jerry," Jimmie said, somewhat shakily. "My balance isn't any too good yet. It's going to be six months before they even let me drive a car. But thank you all for coming. Have a blast."

"And now," Jerry said, "Greg Carmichael will entertain us." Carmichael strode to a wooden church-style lectern ordinarily used by the minister. Glasses clinked.

"We'd better get the food ready," Nina said. "They're gonna need it."

We went into a staff break room, a side room on this floor, not the basement where the deceased were processed. There was only a coffee machine, a tiny refrigerator, and a microwave. No oven or cooktop. Gretzka apparently had already scoped all this out, which was why we had been told to bring everything ready to serve, cold foods first, hot foods at the last minute, completely cooked at Spenser and Angelotti. The white van had two warming ovens, a refrigerator, and a small freezer inside, so there was no fear of the beef roasts cooling off or the sorbets melting.

There were speakers in the break room, feeding in the events from the auditorium. Presumably, the Underhill brothers kept track of what was happening when they had an actual funeral under way. That left them able to rush in if a loved one collapsed or two relatives came to blows, and they'd know when the minister was winding down to a close.

It also meant we could hear the humorist.

The humorist, Carmichael, said, *"Second-hand tombstone for sale. Bargain to a family named Kelly."*

The crowd roared.

Nina poured the container of special Spenser and Angelotti dressing on the avocado and orange sections salad, then tossed it "very gently" as Paul-Michel had unnecessarily reminded her.

Carmichael said, *"My wife makes great soup, but I'll miss her."*

Shaking my head, I gently lifted a portion of salad onto each of forty-four small plates. This was absolutely as close to chef work as I was allowed to go.

"How do you save the life of a man who is at death's door?" The fellow allowed only a split second for anybody to guess, probably knowing somebody would.

"Tell him the cost of a funeral!"

I carried eight plates at a time on a tray into the room with the card tables, managing not to spill anything.

"Then there was the tombstone paid for by a vengeful wife: 'Rest in peace—'"

They all yelled, "'—until we meet again.'"

73

I took out eight more plates. Why tell jokes if everybody knows the punch line?

"*You've heard about the man whose first wife died from eating poison mushrooms. Second wife died from eating poison mushrooms. Third wife died from a skull fracture.*"

Somebody yelled, "*Why a skull fracture?*"

They all screamed in unison, "*She wouldn't eat the poison mushrooms!*"

Now I knew what they were doing. This was the oldest group-cohesion technique in the world. The shared favorite story. Bards and troubadours and a lot of cops I knew did the same thing. As I spooned hot, creamy horseradish sauce into eleven serving bowls, one for each table, I kept an ear cocked to the speaker.

"*I came upon a weeping woman in the cemetery. She was sobbing inconsolably over a grave. 'Why did you die? Why, oh why, did you die?' she sobbed. I felt so sorry for her, I went over and asked, 'Who are you mourning?'*

"*Gasping with grief, she said, 'My husband's first wife.'*"

Nina would carve the huge roasts at the table. This was always a popular presentation.

Because there was no oven here, Gretzka had decided not to include the Spenser and Angelotti specialty Yorkshire pudding with the roast beef and horseradish sauce. Instead, Richard would be rushing over with piping hot onion flat bread when we phoned him that the undertakers were about to sit down. Spenser and Angelotti was two miles away, and Richard would have a tiered hot box in the car.

It was the kind of thing pizzas are transported in, with multiple shallow shelves and a small heater inside. Because of the tiered shelves, the catering gang called it "the jukebox."

From the speaker came: *"A cannibal loves his fellow man. With gravy."*

Then I heard, *"This is the oldest joke in the brotherhood."*

I said to Nina, "I think they're coming to the end."

"They'd better. They sound like they need a gallon of coffee."

We heard: *"A man's mother-in-law dies. The undertaker asks, should we embalm, cremate, or bury her?"*

And all together, the guests screamed, *"He says, 'All three! Take no chances!' "*

Then we heard the stamping of feet. I reached for the cell phone and said, "Richard? Now." Nina reached for the crab rémoulade appetizer.

As Aunt Grace, the same one I mentioned before, would have said, "A good time was had by all." My friend, *Chicago Today* editor Hal Briskman, who loves antique slang, would have called it a "bun fight."

The drinks room had been tidied while the dinner was in rousing progress. Our staff was now in the "dining room" stripping the white cloths from the tables, folding the card tables, and packing the padded china containers with rinsed dishes.

As the last guest lurched out, tacking into a nonexistent side wind, Jimmie and Jerry came over to me.

Jerry said, "That was a wonderful dinner. The chocolate raspberry torte, mmm-mmm-mmm—say, you don't have any left over, do you?"

I laughed. "It's on the shelf in the robing room."

"But put it into a refrigerator *soon*," Nina said, ever the careful chef.

The two brothers resembled each other closely. Their heads were shaped like eggs, pinkly bald on top, with a fringe of limp brown hair ringing the sides and back like a furry horseshoe. Jerry probably was older. He was slightly more wrinkled. Jimmie had more gray in his hair, but I suspected the stress of the accident had contributed to that. Both were slender and tall.

Jimmie said, "I hope you don't think we giggle this way at actual death."

"No. I understand that a celebration is a celebration."

"Yes," he said thoughtfully, "and more. There's a feeling in our profession of being, you know, outsiders."

"I can imagine that."

"Our father was an undertaker. He had his own establishment. And at school, we always got joked at about how the house-guests at our place were a pretty dead bunch. Whatever."

Jerry said, "People don't want to know funeral directors."

Jimmie said, "It was even hard to get dates in school."

Jerry said, "I used to be scared to wear dark suits when I went to school events—"

Jimmie said, "It's really just not easy at all. You meet somebody—"

"They say they're a lawyer or an auto mechanic, whatever, and then they ask what do you do," Jerry said.

"And when you tell them they go, 'Yuk!' " Jimmie said.

I said, "So, I guess the guys who were here tonight, they've all had to deal with that."

"The only people who understand us is other people like us."

I said, "Sure. That makes for a real sense of camaraderie."

"It's comfortable. It's the one time you can kind of let go."

"This wasn't your father's place, then?"

"No, he died while we were too young to be in the business. We were still in school. So we opened later."

"Why don't you call it 'Underhill's' instead of 'The Brothers'?"

They looked at each other and half smiled.

"Too explicit," they said, almost in unison.

✧ 9 ✧

"Salt and pepper to taste."

As we trooped back to the store, my feet were in worse condition than the pickled pigs' feet in deli. I felt like somebody had rolled my eyeballs in breading mix and my usually reliable legs had turned into boiled linguini. How did these people do this day after day? And so cheerfully?

"What was Friday night's event?" I asked Nina.

"Oh, that was such a hoot! Wish you'd been there."

"Did Gretzka go?"

"Yeah. Of course."

"But Cartier didn't go to these things tonight."

Nina frowned, wondering how much to tell me. I waited. If you let the person think a few seconds, you're more likely to get answers than if you push.

Finally she said, "Serge Gretzka is well paid, but he works hard for it. He goes to almost every event we do. I'm the chef, which means I cook, I carve, I flambé, I do the on-site crêpes suzette, I stir-fry. But he makes sure everything is there and is right." She paused again. "Not like Cartier. Serge isn't at all like Cartier."

"So why was Friday night a hoot?"

"It was the monthly meeting of some Chicago mystery writers. And one of the writers pushed another writer down the steps."

"You're kidding!"

"It started during cocktails," she said. "Some sort of argument about *punctuation,* if you can believe that." She giggled. "But I was tossing the stir-fry veggies and didn't hear much of it."

"And?"

"Everything seemed fine. We were there right through the lecture or speech or whatever. On how to kill people with poisons, as if they needed to hear that during dinner, but these are weird people and, anyhow, I was flaming the crêpes for dessert, so we cleaned up while the speech was ending, and we left at the same time as everybody else did."

"And?"

"Well, Serge was walking out next to this woman who had had the argument with this man—"

"And—"

"And when they started down the steps, she suddenly shot forward headfirst! Can you believe?"

Nina Timko's boyfriend had been waiting for her in the parking lot when we arrived, so she moved fast to clean up and leave. When she opened the back door of the deli/catering kitchen, he was outside, leaning on the wall, waiting for her. "This is Gregory," she said. "Gregory, meet Cat." And she was off.

Two staffers remained at Spenser and Angelotti to put pans to soak and to fill four restaurant-size dishwashers with all the crockery and serving utensils we brought back. Nina, being a chef, never did pans, apparently. Paul-Michel Cartier had left by 10 P.M., when he knew that the food had all arrived at the Underhills' safely and was hot, right, and enough.

I walked out into the gigantic store. It was dim but studded with safety lights throughout. The time was now 11 P.M. In less than an hour the cleanup people would be out of here. Everybody said that was typical. Everybody out by midnight, usually; nobody back in the store until 5 A.M., when the early bakers arrived. Dough was rising in the bakery in three different temperature-controlled "closets."

The aisles of canned goods were very dark. Far away to my right, the fruit department was nearly dark as well, the neat piles of cantaloupes only highlighted and looking like babies' heads.

The checkout lanes were much more brightly lit. So was the meat department. A police car could swing through the parking lot outside and see most of the public part of the store. Presumably they would notice if a gang was looting the place. But the nonpublic areas were not visible.

I turned and went back through the "authorized personnel only" door and into the silent hall that led to the workrooms and offices. This hall ran from north to south, down the entire length of the enormous building, dividing the public part of the store from the behind-the-scenes part. Back here, on the east side of the hall, were all the work areas. From north to south in order were Spenser's office at the extreme north, Angelotti's office next, the accounting office where the huge stock-management computing system also lived, the personnel office, the staff lounge or break room, the catering office, the bakery, the deli/catering kitchen, two staff bathrooms, the butcher shop, and, last, at the south end, a huge storage space, divided into a part for semi-perishables, such as vegetables and fruit, and a part for non-perishables like canned goods. I was standing in front of the doors into the large deli and catering kitchens. I turned right to study the distance to the butcher shop, which was two-thirds of the way down, just short of the big storeroom.

Staring, deep in thought, toward the butcher shop end in the silent, dim hall, I gasped when a hand fell on my shoulder.

"Aaaahhhh! Jeez!" I said, with some justification.

"Oh, did I startle you?" It was Henry Spenser.

"You practically caused cardiac collapse and death."

"I'm sorry." But he didn't look sorry. He looked annoyed at the world.

"Mr. Spenser, I know you're having a hard couple of days."

"I'm having a lot more than that. I've been going over the figures for hours. We're losing a ton of money on this recall. Horrible, horrible losses. And total sales today are down

81

significantly from a normal Sunday. Naturally. Who wants to buy food at a store that has to recall it because there's something bad in it?"

He was carrying a briefcase, I noticed. His office door at the end of the hall was open and dark. The door had been closed half a minute earlier.

"Mr. Spenser, do you often work late?"

"Late. Not this late."

"Oh."

"And I didn't work late Friday night, to answer the question you were going to ask. I left at ten o'clock. If I had been here late, to answer your next question, yes, I would have noticed lights in the butcher area, assuming they were on. And I would have investigated."

"You don't leave lights on in the butcher shop?"

"Only a safety light."

"If there had been a killer in the butcher shop, and you'd been in your office, he wouldn't have seen your office light. It doesn't show around the door."

"I leave my door open when I go home."

"So does Mr. Angelotti, I see. Anybody would know you were both gone, then, if the doors were both open."

"Right. They could assume that."

"What are your security arrangements?"

"I'll show you."

We went back into the public part of the store and stood in the central aisle.

"The front doors are locked every night when we close at nine P.M., except Saturday, when it's ten. The janitors clean the sales floor between nine and eleven. The two side fire doors are always locked from outside, day and night, and the panic bar will always open them from inside, day and night. If the panic bar is pushed, an alarm rings in the store and in the local fire department. The alarm company then calls my home and Bruno's home and also dispatches a runner."

"Got it. So I shouldn't wander out the fire doors."

He shook his head. He wasn't feeling like smiling. "There's a huge sign on each fire door to make sure nobody uses it by mistake."

"Got it."

"It happens about twice a year anyway. People!"

They are a troublesome factor in life, I thought.

"You're aware of the back delivery doors and the doors into the work areas. You can work late in the bakery, deli, catering, or butcher areas and leave by those back doors. They lock behind you when you go out."

"Can they be opened from outside?"

"Yes, but only by key."

"All night?"

"Yes. Day or night. But those doors only. The front doors will sound an alarm if anybody goes in them or out through them between eleven P.M. and seven A.M. *no matter what.* Even if you have a key. If I wanted to let anybody in through the front doors during those hours, I would have to disarm the entire system."

"Makes sense. Nobody who works here at night needs to use the front doors."

"Exactly."

"Who has keys to get in the back doors?"

"Bruno, me, three bakers, two butchers, both deli managers, the two chefs, Harry Kennelly and Nina Timko. Four janitorial people. Two secretaries. One bookkeeper."

"Eighteen people. That's a lot."

"Yes and no. They have to get in and we know who they are. You also need to be aware, Ms. Marsala, that no significant money is left here overnight. The bookkeeper takes all the cash that's come in plus all checks to the bank every day at eight P.M. for night deposit. We leave enough to make change first thing in the morning. It's a fair amount, and I'd hate to lose it, but it's not a fortune. As far as the store's contents, I suppose a trusted employee with a key might drive up in a truck, back the truck up to the loading doors that give entry to the storerooms, and try to strip the store, but they'd run into two problems."

"What are they?" He wanted me to ask.

"First, the security cameras. He or they would be videotaped. There are two focused on the exterior of the loading dock and two inside the storerooms."

"Do any focus on the other exits, like the butcher shop?"

"No."

"Suppose an intruder broke the cameras? Or sprayed the lenses with black paint?"

"They didn't on Friday or Saturday night. Your chief McCoo has the tapes. And even if somebody disabled the cameras, they'd still trip the alarm system." He pointed down the aisle of canned soup. "You see that thing on the wall? It looks like a fire alarm box."

"Near the Evian rack? Yes."

"It generates an infrared beam that shoots to—" He turned and pointed all the way across the store to a spot on the farthest wall over a cold case of cheeses. "Shoots to a receiver over there. The beam is turned on when the alarm is set for the evening. If the beam is broken, the alarm sounds in the store and the alarm company is immediately notified, et cetera, et cetera, et cetera, just like the fire doors."

"I see."

"There are two of those crisscrossing the store at about chest height. If you walk through here after I set the system, you will break one of those beams. Also, at the corners and the midpoint of the walls, mounted high on the walls for good coverage, are eight motion detectors. Motion detectors don't have as long a range as the beams. Between the two types, they cover the store."

"By the store, you mean the public areas?"

"The marketing areas. Yes, but there's more." He marched back through the "authorized personnel only" door, apparently assuming I'd follow him. He was right, too.

We were now in the hall that accessed the offices and the bakery, deli and catering kitchens, butcher shop, and storerooms. He pointed to another set of infrared beam sender and receiver and a motion detector.

"These cover the entire length of the hall."

"I can see that." The beam sender was next to his office door, the receiver at the other end. "So what we're saying is that when you or Bruno leave for the night—"

"We set these. Right."

"And nobody can get into the store—the marketing area—or into this hall, without setting off the system."

"Exactly."

"But they can get into the butcher area."

"And bakery and so on. Yes. But only certain people who have a key."

I thought about that for a while. The killer wouldn't really have needed to get into the store or the offices. In fact, there was no evidence he or she had been anywhere but the butcher shop. And he wouldn't need to get out through the front doors. No point. He could leave by the back butcher shop door, and it would lock after him when it closed. Nobody would ever know he'd been there.

"Mr. Spenser, say there are eighteen people, including you and Bruno, who had permission to be here after hours and had keys to certain doors. How many people didn't have keys, but at least knew how the system worked?"

That displeased him. "We don't keep our procedures secret. This isn't a bank, you know. Or a doctor's office with drugs that people are desperate to steal."

"I'm not criticizing. I just want to get a picture."

"A *lot*, Ms. Marsala. Check-out people, stock people. Even our regular delivery people. Plumbers. Electrical contractors. Hundreds. Especially if you stop to think that we hire a lot of young people who work part-time, and temporaries as checkouts and bag handlers. Over the years, maybe a thousand or more."

I thought about that as we stood there, facing each other in the hall. "Mr. Spenser—"

"Yes?"

"You didn't want Mr. Angelotti to hire me."

"You're an unnecessary expense."

"I don't want to be at cross-purposes with you. I want to help."

"The police can do their job without help."

"Ordinarily, yes. If they find some really useful trace evidence. Or if somebody out there who knows something comes forward. Suppose there aren't any traces or any witnesses or any friends of the killer just waiting to blow the whistle? I might hear something the police wouldn't."

"A fair number of murderers are never caught."

"I can't believe you want that to happen."

"My concern is the survival of the store. I very much hope that what took place here is never known by the public."

"Well, I can understand that."

"And having you ask questions makes it more likely that one of our staff might begin to suspect something."

"I'm very careful."

"I hope so. I doubt total caution is possible, if you're digging for answers."

"Mr. Angelotti believes that getting to the bottom of what happened is best for the store in the long run."

"Mr. Angelotti—uh, is a genius. I mean that. Not only is he a man with a real palate, and a brilliant cook, both skilled and inventive—an artist—but he has a sense of what foods people are *going to be* interested in. Almost as if he knew what would tickle their taste buds next."

"But?"

"But he has no sense of business. As far as money is concerned, he's a child."

When I did the article on Spenser and Angelotti six months ago, I had emphasized the differences between the two men. Henry Spenser had grown up in Winnetka, one of the most expensive suburbs north of Chicago. He had gone to Yale, followed by the business school at Northwestern University, followed by ten years at a Fortune 500 company where he was rising in the ranks. Rising higher and higher, but not enjoying it. He wanted his own business.

Bruno Angelotti, on the other hand, had grown up in Italy, a child during World War II, and essentially a displaced person, as war refugees used to be called, for many years after that. His parents, along with his mother's mother, had settled in Queens, a borough of

New York City. They had chickens in their backyard, and so did their Italian neighbors. They were people who understood where food really came from.

Bruno told me about his grandmother cutting the heads off chickens for Sunday dinner. If you didn't cut low enough on the neck, some of the brain stem was left. And the chicken would go running around the yard "like a chicken with its head cut off."

So it was no surprise to me when I saw that Bruno wanted all kinds of products from around the world, including dried squid and whole eels, that looked like what they were. I thought it was charming when he showed me around the store and actually winced at the aisle of bright-colored soda pop and the aisle of packaged candy, and hurried me past the sugary breakfast cereals. But he lingered with delight at the row of fresh strawberries, raspberries, and blueberries. Or the cases of cracked ice nestled with seaweedy clams and mussels, and whole catfish, eyeballs and all.

Nor was it any surprise that Henry Spenser wanted to display the pieces of meat in sterile, impersonal packages. Beef that seemed never to have seen a cow. Fish fillets that never needed eyes or fins. Chicken that arose out of nowhere as drumsticks or boned breasts.

"Do you know that fewer and fewer people every year buy whole chickens for roasting?" Spenser said to me. "They want parts. Impersonal. No guilt. In packages with sterile wrapping."

And once when I got to their offices early, I heard Spenser and Angelotti having an argument.

Spenser was saying, "It'll ruin us."

"No it won't, Henry," Bruno said. "Five new cheeses? How can that ruin us?"

"We have a hundred and four types of cheese as of last week. We don't need any more."

"People come here because we have everything."

"Every time you increase the number of items we carry, you increase costs. Stocking costs, supervisory costs, accounting costs, let alone with perishables there's wastage. Do you realize that we have to throw out twenty-seven percent of our cheese because it goes past sale date!"

"That's not important."

"It is *very* important! I can tell you exactly how much it costs us per month. I have it right here—"

"Henry, it is *not important*! All that is important is that we have every food anyone might want, and that everything we have is all of the best. If we are not known all over Chicago as the very best, we are just another store, struggling desperately to compete with every other ordinary supermarket. Six-packs of Coke at ten percent off. A sale on toilet tissue. We have no expertise for that and no reason to think that's a battle we can win!"

That was six months ago. Would their disagreement have gone away? Or grown worse?

Anyway, about midnight I found myself

alone in the butcher shop. It was dimly lit, like the rest of the store. I wasn't entirely alone; the people washing pans in the deli/catering kitchen were just putting away the last of the equipment.

As I noticed the first time I saw it, the working area of a modern butcher shop has much in common with a surgical suite, a pathology lab, or the morgue. A path lab has microscopes, of course, and these days a lot of high-tech machines, and the surgical suite has a lot of monitoring gadgets, but those are the major differences. The similarities are everywhere: The main decor element is stainless steel. Stainless steel implements, tools, shelves, doors, rolling tables, stationary tables. The light is bright, and every corner is illuminated. It is also very uninteresting light, broad spectrum, as close to daylight as electricity can produce. The actual color of meat is as important to a butcher for judging its quality as the color of a person's skin is to a doctor judging his physical condition.

The floor is seamless. The idea for labs and operating rooms and butcher shops is that the floor should be able to be quickly and thoroughly cleaned. Many of them, including this one, now have a poured floor-covering, much like the rolled composite that is laid down in one flat swath, but this is mixed and poured on the spot. The result is no seams whatsoever. Nothing to trap dirt. Or blood.

Another similarity—the ventilation is good. Most of the time you don't smell much of anything.

And of course, they all have a lot of sharp things lying around.

Okay, I said to myself, I'm a killer.

The butcher area was large, possibly twenty by thirty feet. There were sausage stuffers with tubelike ends, huge slicers that fed roasts and turkey rolls and bologna and so on into rotating blades, grinders, and choppers for grinding lamb, turkey, beef, and sausage stuffing. There were odd implements such as larding needles, long hollow things that you stick into roasts to insert strips of fat. And, of course, tables—cutting tables, rolling tables, chopping block tables. And a fleet of rolling racks, open shelving for moving the finished product to the marketing floor.

Why kill here?

Why? Why leave the bones? Why package them?

Well, the easiest answer to why kill here is that here was where they were, the killer and the victim, when one attacked the other. Either they both worked here, or one did and met the other here after hours. Either one of them planned to kill the other here, or this was where they got into an argument. Why here? One of them worked here; I was certain of it.

The why of everything else, though, was not so clear.

I walked around the periphery of the room. At one end were the three large walk-in coolers. I tried to open them, but they were locked. Ordinary key locks, not combination, and no obvious sign of an alarm. The east wall held the back doors and a long row of storage shelves. The south wall held a bathroom and storage shelves. I opened the bathroom door. It had the usual items inside, but over the sink was an upside-down bottle of disinfectant soap, and both over the sink and on the inside of the door were signs reading: WASH HANDS BEFORE RETURNING TO WORK!

The west wall, which backed up to the access corridor, was work space, mainly cutting tables, and the fourth was racks and sinks. The whole center space was standing equipment.

I'm the killer and I'm here with a body. Everybody else has left work for the day. I can peek into the hall and see that Angelotti and Spenser have both left, since their doors are open, but I can't go into the hall because of the motion detector and IR beam. I can see by their red lights that the devices are on. My choice is to stay here in a closed room and do what has to be done, or to take the body away.

If I were the killer I'd be terribly afraid to take the body away. There'd be nothing more terrifying than to be in my car with a body in the back, wondering if I'd be stopped by a cop or get into an accident or have a breakdown.

I'd dispose of the body right here, if I could.

Any way I could.

I left by the double back doors, even though my car was around in front. The back parking lot was very narrow, unlike the huge front lot. A driveway led past the back of the store, wide enough to accommodate big delivery trucks.

The lighting back here was that peach-colored stuff that makes you look like you have yellow fever. There were a couple of cars parked in the narrow lot, and beyond them traffic roared past on Armitage Avenue.

It was pretty obvious that if a killer walked out these doors at, say, 4 A.M., nobody would notice. The people in the cars driving by on Armitage might see him, but they'd be comparatively few at that hour and too far away to pick up any detail. And anyway, why would they care?

I rounded the south side of the store, checking as I always do for muggers, murderers, and the dangerously loony. There weren't any.

My car was under the nice light pole where I had left it, the one that was labeled D9 JUST ARRIVED—CHILEAN POMPANO FILLETS. I glanced underneath, to check for homicidal maniacs.

Pathetically grateful to be going home, I zapped the lock, opened the door, glanced behind the seat for more homicidal maniacs, backed onto the seat, and swung my tired legs into the car.

And crunched.

There were diamonds all over the front seat.

Except that they weren't diamonds and they were going to cost me. The whole windshield had been smashed.

I drove home extra slowly, so that the wind through the broken windshield didn't dry my eyeballs out or whip dust into them. How do people drive those motorcycles without windshields? Goggles, probably. As if that wasn't bad enough, my message machine held six business-related messages and two nonbusiness.

My mother's voice said, "Call me when you get in, dear." "Dear" meant she was going to tell me to do something.

My sister-in-law, Roxanne, said, "Your mother is going to be calling you. After you talk with her, call me *before you do another thing*!"

Don't you love it?

"Hello, Mom?"

"You're calling rather late."

"You said to call the minute I got in. And it's not that late."

"You haven't responded to my last message."

"Your fifty-fifth wedding anniversary party? I wanted to be sure I didn't have an obligation—"

"You can't have, dear. This is important."

"But you just had that big fiftieth and that was only five years ago." Like, great math, Cat.

"This is twice as important."

"But the fiftieth is the golden—twice fifty is a hundred—wait, why twice?"

"It has two fives."

"What? That's not what makes it twice—"

"Anyway, I want you to pick up Teddy, so we'll be sure he's there. Teddy is so hard to be sure of."

Teddy is my youngest brother. I have a zillion brothers, but Teddy is the only one younger than I am. And the only one I am really close to. Teddy got into a whole lot of trouble when he was nineteen and actually went to jail for it. But he's all right now. I hope I hope.

"Well, okay, Mom. I'll try to get him."

Which meant I had just agreed I'd be there, too.

"Roxanne?"

"Cat? Well, at last!" Roxanne always sounded rushed but in fact had too little to occupy her mind and had not worked outside the home since five unfortunate months in 1982 with Pesky Telemarketers.

"It can't have been that long since you called. Your message was after Mom's."

"Now listen, I know she asked you to bring Teddy."

"Well, yes."

"Don't."

"Don't? Roxanne, he's her son!"

"Just pretend you never got hold of him."

"What's this all about?"

"We have some business associates coming to the party, it's at ever such a nice place, and you know how Teddy looks. His hair is down to his shoulders, and he never shaves. It's disgusting!"

"Disgusting? Roxanne, that three-day growth of beard is a much-favored Hollywood fashion statement. Although I never could figure out how they did it without ever having a one-day growth or a four-day growth—"

"Cat, we don't want him there."

"*We?* Who we? Why are you worrying about this nonissue?"

"Nonissue? I don't want these people to think we have family members who look like that."

"This is Mom's life, here. I am not going to finagle a way of keeping her own son from her own party, Roxanne. It would be cruel."

"Besides, Douglas says so."

"Dougie?" Her husband. My second-oldest brother.

"Douglas," she said.

And what Dougie says goes, I suppose. Dougie is the boss in this family.

"I'll see what I can do." And what I could do was bring Teddy. As he was.

97

✧ 10 ✧

"Select several meaty tomatoes, preferably plum tomatoes, such as Roma or San Marzano. Dip in boiling water for seven seconds. Peel, seed, and chop."

"He's not there," Bruno moaned, holding his head in his hands.

I said, "Who's not where?"

"Serge Gretzka. He never arrived in Panama City."

"Oh. Oh-oh."

"I told the police I couldn't get him on the phone, you know. As you said to. They asked the Panama City police to go to the condo."

"And they didn't find him?"

"Or his wife. They never arrived."

"Oh, my God."

It was eight-thirty Monday morning. I had come in early, entering by the back doors because the front weren't open yet. There turned out to be an outside bell that delivery people could ring. Dack had come and let me in. Wonderful smells wafted from the bakery. Pretending to go to the catering office, I had tapped on Bruno's door and slipped inside.

"So let me get this straight," I said. "He was going with his wife to Florida for his vacation."

"Yes."

"And neither one of them has been heard of since Friday evening?"

"Right."

"Did you phone his house here in Chicago?"

"Yes. No answer."

"What kind of a person is this Gretzka?"

"Oh, a wonderful man," Bruno said in his slight accent. "A talented cook, and just a perfect person for the job of catering manager. Good at finding out what would really please a client. What kind of foods would thrill a customer who needed glamour. He could tell when a group wanted something simple and ample, and when they wanted something flamboyantly spectacular and when they wanted something artistic and new and different. If he's—if he's gone for any, oh, dear heaven, any reason whatever, I just don't know how we could ever replace him."

"Personally, in his private life, what is he like?"

"Oh, lovely, a lovely man."

"Well, but does he have enemies? Do people here in the store envy him?"

"I doubt it. I think they admire him."

"Even the assistant catering manager? Paul-Michel Cartier? He doesn't want to take Gretzka's place?"

"Oh, I don't think so. We're all friends here."

Sure they are. Like this is the only place on earth without envy and competition. "Bruno, I have to ask. What is Gretzka's relationship with his wife?"

"Just fine. Wonderful, I think. Sophie has

99

no relatives, I think, so they depend on each other."

"He doesn't make advances to the women in the store? The cashiers, maybe?" Bruno was shaking his head. "The olive oil lady? Nina Timko? Anybody's wife?"

"Absolutely not! Serge is a very moral man."

I gave it up. If there was going to be gossip, it wasn't going to come from this office. For a few seconds I wondered whether I should tell him about my windshield being broken. But there was no good reason to. It could easily have been done by some passing lout, of which there seems to be an ample supply. And while I was furious last night when I called the police to report the damage so that my insurance would cover it, and even more furious this morning as I drove with the wind in my face to D&G Auto Glass While-U-Wait "One Hour Service All Charge Cards We'll Meet Any Price," there was no proof it was Bruno's problem. Wouldn't hurt to wait.

"Do the Spenser and Angelotti people get together socially?"

"Well, of course. We have company parties. Cater them ourselves, too. Wonderful parties."

"And wonderful food, I'm sure. I suppose there was no irregularity in money going into the catering department?"

"No money goes into the catering department. The events are paid by check or charge card directly to the company. Except maybe tips at the events, anything customers want to give out themselves. Small amounts."

"Oh, but, Bruno. You know people can finagle. Take one example: product rip-offs. Gretzka could make five roasts of beef and sell one. He could say it took twenty bottles of champagne to serve a crowd, when it only took fifteen, and he could sell the rest."

Bruno sighed. "Yes, and it was for this kind of thinking that I wanted you to come here, so I can't complain. But I must tell you, Cat, that I do not believe this of Serge. Not only is he an unusually ethical person, his amounts are always just about what I would expect for the event. The customers are always happy with quantities, so there is no undersupply. No running out. I just can't imagine what you suggest."

"Well, okay."

"There is one thing that bothers me, though."

"What's that?"

"Serge asked me a question a few days before he left. He asked, quite casually, you see, what the regulations were for disposal of dead bodies."

"We're doing just the one lunch today," Paul-Michel said.

Apparently Monday was a slow day in catering. Very rarely did anyone give Monday night parties, and even business lunches were more common toward the end of the week.

I said, "So who's this for?"

"A law firm. Sadler and Weiser."

"What's the occasion?"

101

"They've just hired a batch of baby lawyers. It's a welcome to the firm."

"Hmm. How long will Mr. Gretzka be on vacation?"

"Two weeks. Why?"

Why indeed. "Just wondering. I want to keep my job after he gets back."

"Well, do your work properly and we'll see."

"Is Mr. Gretzka an exacting man?"

"We both are."

"Will I like him?" I meant, of course, "Do you like him?" But I was trying to be slick.

"Yes. Now make sure they've loaded the rum for the flambé. And check that they have matches. Once they had to ask a client for a cigarette lighter. Very bad form. Sometimes they just don't *think*!"

Hey, they may have presented a picture of one big happy family, but you can't tell me that dozens and dozens of people all working together are all going to love one another. I wish, but I don't believe. Some of them are going to have to boss others around, just in the nature of the work. Some of them are going to be working on the same level of the hierarchy and therefore competing with each other for promotion. Some will fall in love. Or in hate.

"Nina," I said, "what sort of person is Mr. Gretzka?"

"Okay, I guess."

"That's not very enthusiastic."

I was lighting the solid-fuel pots under the serving pans in the law firm's conference room. We have enough chafing dishes and *bain-marie* pans to serve the entire Sixth Fleet. Yesterday I didn't even know what a *bain-marie* was. It's a form of double boiler. It's a container that holds simmering hot water. A matching container of food is set into it to stay hot without burning.

Sadler and Weiser went in for marble. We came up in the service elevator, but were allowed to pass through the entry hall once to go to a storeroom to collect some napery with the firm logo on it. The whole entry wall was white marble lightly veined with pale green, into which the firm's name had been deeply chiseled. They were a seventy-five-partner firm, medium large for Chicago, with a hundred secretaries, fifty paralegals, ninety associates, and the cause of the celebration, forty "new hires." We were providing a buffet for all of them, who were excused at staggered times, of course, because somebody had to be minding the store.

We now stood in front of a curving wall of black marble veined with white in an enormous conference room. The windows looked out at the Loop and beyond it, Lake Michigan. We wore our white uniforms with little red-and-white-check aprons.

"What does Gretzka look like?"

"Medium tall. Nice-looking, if you like the type."

"What type is that?"

"Oh, dark. Dark eyes. Dark hair. Big fore-head with bulgy temples. Big shoulders."

"Do you think Gretzka would have con-taminated the meat?" I asked Nina, somewhat deceptively.

"Oh, heavens no!"

"Why not?"

"Sabotage Spenser and Angelotti! No *way*! He's prissy. Oh, that's not fair. He isn't exactly prissy, but particular. Everything just so."

"Well, that doesn't mean he couldn't go nuts."

"You ask me, people go seriously nuts in ways that they were already medium nuts."

"I think that's very wise."

"Of course, he *could* get jealous."

"Jealous?" Tell me more.

"Well, yeah. What with Nicholas Lane after his wife."

❖ 11 ❖

"Scatter the chopped tomatoes, basil, thyme, and cracked pepper over the meat in the casserole."

What a great method of murder! I thought. Say Gretzka is smoldering with anger. Day after day, he wonders where his wife is while he's at work. What is she doing? In the nature of things, he will be on the job a lot in evenings and on weekends. Nicholas Lane is the head baker. He works a regular eight hours. He starts early, to be sure; he usually works 5 A.M. to 1 P.M., with no overtime to speak of. He gets off early.

How many times would Gretzka pass the bakery in the later afternoon and see it shut down, and wonder where Lane was and what he was doing? And was he doing it with Sophie? Gretzka was described as a very moral, upright man. He would be hurt, violated, and angry.

How many times would Gretzka be flaming the cherries jubilee at a catered event, burning inside with fury?

And when finally he couldn't stand it any longer, did he tell his wife to come and pick him up after work on Friday night, knowing everybody would be out by twelve? "We have to finish packing for the trip, dear. You use the car today but pick me up tonight. Ring the bell. I won't be finished until twelve-thirty, because I have to leave detailed instructions for everybody. Maybe one A.M. would be even better."

One A.M. arrives. Everybody is long gone. The store is deserted except for Gretzka. Sophie rings the buzzer near the back door and Gretzka lets her in. He strikes her on the head, killing her, and then begins dismembering the body. The soft parts go down the disposals or toilet. Even small bones.

The teeth might clog the plumbing. He decides to carry those away, because they

105

won't take up much space. He'll dispose of them later. The clothes? Well, that's a harder problem. Can't leave them here, can't be seen here with women's clothes, even if they're only a little bloody. Well, dump them on any run-down street and hope somebody would find them and take them home to use, rather than call the police.

But the large bones couldn't be ground up; they are much too hard. In the bone barrel they might catch somebody's eye. Large beef bones are always sold for soup, never thrown out. All right, package them. It's automated; it's easy. So he cuts the bones into normal sales sizes and runs them through the automated packager.

Finished with the grisly process, he leaves.

He carries away her clothing, which is not particularly suspicious if he is stopped by police for a traffic violation or gets in an accident. And her teeth, which are small enough to conceal in a pocket. And probably hair.

He "and his wife" leave for "Florida" the next morning, but he actually goes somewhere else. Assuming everybody believes they are together, maybe he will send a message toward the end of his two-week vacation that he has decided to take a job in Florida. That he's hired a broker to sell his house. "My wife and I are just tired of those Chicago winters."

Gretzka would not know his deed had been discovered, since word of the murder was not out.

And that's a good reason, too, for us to keep it quiet for now.

And with that, Sophie Gretzka would effectively vanish. As Bruno had told me, she had no other relatives to ask after her.

Gretzka would have vanished his wife.

"McCoo," I said, "have your people searched the sewers around Spenser and Angelotti for teeth?"

"It's standard to search the sewers. If they found teeth, they'd be right in here telling me about it."

"Or hair?"

"Or hair."

"Oh. Well, I hope they cast a wide enough net."

Not deigning to answer that, McCoo said, "This is Costa Rican." He poured me a generous cup of his new coffee. His wife, Susanne, had just given him some new cups. These were delicate, white and blue porcelain. I held mine over my head to look at the brand, which is very rude, but even as I did so, McCoo said, "Wedgwood."

"Right."

"You'll find this robust, I think. It's a medium roast, not too dark. I'm beginning to think that some of the European dark roasts came about as a response to scarcity. The darker the roast, the more coffee you can brew and still have some oomph. For my favorite beans, I prefer to taste the actual coffee flavor."

"But McCoo, you always liked dark roast."

"Oh, I still do. My tastes are almost universal, as long as the quality is good—the beans properly grown, and roasted not more than seven days before. I've just bought a roaster. Now this particular bean has a rich, nutty aftertaste."

"I just came from food city. I don't think I can talk flavors right now."

"You mean you'd drink coffee that didn't have a pedigree?"

"In a word, yes. Even instant."

"Arrgh! Cat, you have no soul."

"But this coffee is very good. I *do* know the difference. So look, McCoo, I don't have too much time. I need to know two things. First, does anybody at the store have an alibi for Friday night? Or early Saturday morning, whichever you call it."

"No."

"None of them? I can't believe that."

"Believe it. How many people do you know who have witnesses to where they are the whole time between one A.M. and five A.M.?"

"Some people must. Bruno is married, isn't he?"

"Sure. He and his wife went to bed at eleven. His wife says he was there all night. They live ten blocks from the store. She was sound asleep all night. What good is that? The other people who work at the store mostly work days. They sleep nights."

"Okay, okay. I also need to know what the techs found out about the butcher shop area. I suppose it's asking too much for you to call them and tell them to talk with me."

108

"Are you kidding? You could blackmail me out of my house and my new coffee roaster right now."

"I could?"

"With the exception of your friend Sam, you're the only civilian who knows Chicago's darkest secret. Hizzoner wants to extend the twenty-four-hour info black-out." From his voice I knew he was still annoyed with the mayor.

"Oh. That's true. Gives me a lot of power, huh?"

"Well, if the cops or techs or MEs leak the word, they can be fired. You we can't do anything about."

"Ha! I love that."

"The mayor is *very* serious about keeping this quiet. You could probably blackmail *him* out of his box seats at Comiskey Park. He has visions of Chicago being the next Milwaukee."

"What do you mean?"

"Well, you remember when all those people in Milwaukee were getting sick from the water? There was bacterial runoff from hog farms or something like that in the drinking water. And this was right after Jeffrey Dahmer was caught cannibalizing people. The joke was, 'In Milwaukee you can eat the people but you can't drink the water.' "

"Right. I do remember."

"Can you imagine where the stand-up comics would go with this? Already my detective, Torvil, said to me, 'This certainly makes you wonder about head cheese.' "

"That's truly awful."

"'Or Irish stew.'"

"Please!"

"Yeah, well, imagine if there were professional jokesters on the job. Think of the economic impact. Chicago is known for beef. The Chicago Beef Association, the Meatpackers, the Pork Association, good God, they'd all be trembling in their boots if they heard about this. The mayor is already angry about the number of people who know. He's called three times this morning. I keep telling him that we can't investigate with fewer. And, of course, you can't take knowledge out of the heads of the ones who know now."

"Can you really keep them quiet?"

"Your guess is as good as mine. At least we're not adding anybody. I reswore them to secrecy again today. They've been told they get barbecued if they talk."

"All right, all right. I'm sorry to put it this way, McCoo, but how can I turn this to my advantage?"

"You want to go over to the ME's office? Or down to the lab? I'll give you notes for both. They're not done testing the evidence, though."

"Give me the notes. But I gotta go after work. I'm here on my lunch hour."

"Just as well. They're swamped with trace evidence. If you can call two hundred pounds of ground meat a trace."

"Heat white wine and beef stock sufficient to come halfway up the meat in the casserole."

I took a look at Nicholas Lane. He was a hunk. Blond hair, large shoulders, chiseled profile. Lane was medium tall, moved like a panther, and, as I watched, his strong arms were removing a large two-by-three-foot sheet of double-fudge brownies from the oven. There ought to be a law against gorgeous guys working as bakers. Two temptations in one place was too many.

So was he romancing Sophie Gretzka? And was Dapper's bone part of Sophie?

It had looked like a largish bone, I remembered, as I walked to my desk in the catering office. Sam had thought the bone was from a male, but he didn't know for sure. How big was Sophie?

I said to Nina, "What sort of person is Gretzka's wife?"

"What's this fascination with Gretzka?"

I couldn't think of a single good lie, so I said, "Humor me."

She gave me a very strange look. "Now you're interested in his wife?"

"Well, didn't you meet her at company parties?"

"Yes, sure. Well, she seems very cheerful."

Oh, dear. For some reason it's sadder when happy people die. "And?"

"And actually she seems to like to party. She's kind of ditzy. She flirts. She sure flirted with Nicholas Lane."

"What does she look like?"

"Honestly, you are very weird. She's blonde, really quite pretty. Not exactly beautiful. Too much chin. Too much makeup, too."

"Is she big?"

Nina sighed. "Big? Yes. Tall, anyway, not fat. As tall as Gretzka, and I guess he's about five feet ten."

"Like inferior wines, inferior olive oils may be passed off as those of higher quality," said the olive oil lady. "If you pick up a bottle"—here she picked up a bottle and pointed at the label—"and it says *packed* in Italy, it may have been grown elsewhere and was only, as it says, packed in Italy. Like wines, where you have to look for the words *mise en bouteille au château* for a château-bottled wine, you must look for the words *prodotto ed imbottigliato en Italia* for an oil produced and bottled in Italy."

She had a rapt audience, and you had to admire her, she sounded just as enthusiastic about olive oil today as she had yesterday.

"And don't overlook the excellent oils now being grown in California. They tend to be fruitier than Italian oils, and are quite exciting as a drizzle on grilled fish, bread, or white beans. And so much more healthful than butter."

I had parked in front when I came back from visiting McCoo on my late lunch hour, so I passed the Fern Ffolke, swaying ethereally at the center door. Today they held six placards. Lined up in a row, these placards depicted a little yellow chick, a happy-looking hen, a hen held in man's hairy hand, a hen with its head under a knife, a decapitated hen with blood oozing, and a dead hen being eviscerated.

This must make Henry Spenser absolutely hopping mad.

However, once inside the store, you wouldn't even know the Fern Ffolke were outside. I guess they were being very careful to remain outside, so as not to give the law a reason to get after them for trespass.

I spent the afternoon taking phone calls about catering. Too many were curiosity seekers, asking what the "contamination" was, rather than real customers.

I discussed menus with a woman who wanted to arrange a "lovely dinner for a hundred of our closest friends." Red snapper was good but costly right now, and she liked that. Broiled red snapper, a variety of appetizers including snails in puff pastry, broccoli, salad of tiny new greens, and possibly a tarte aux fraises. I had just hung up when Paul-Michel came in and looked at my notes.

"Are you crazy!" he yelled.

"What did I do wrong?"

"You think you can serve *broccoli* with a delicate fish like red snapper?"

"Well, yeah. Um, yeah. I do. Did."

"Broccoli has a strong, almost harsh taste. You would *never* serve it with a mild fish."

"No. Never again."

"Don't *showboat,* Ms. Marsala. Use the menus as they are, or come to me if you have what you consider to be an idea."

"But she said she liked broccoli."

"Unfortunately, she may have guests with more taste than she has."

"Um, okay."

"Give them baby green peas. No, better yet, snow peas, tiny buttered snow pea pods. They're just coming in now from Georgia. And rice. Possibly cooked with a mild mushroom. Shiitake mushrooms would be acceptable."

"How is your lawyer doing?" I asked Spenser as I passed him in the hall. No one else was nearby.

"Barkley?" He said the name unnecessarily. After all, who else were we talking about? I think he was trying to delay answering, to gain time to think. Finally he said, "Well, actually, he's in the—uh—psychiatric unit at Northwestern."

"Good heavens! Poor man! Well, that's nothing to be ashamed of. I suppose he needed help. But why?"

"Uh—well, actually, you remember he got upset Saturday night when we came to the store."

"Sure I remember."

"He looked at the—you know, evidence. His wife had shopped here that afternoon. She, uh, frankly, she went home and made meatballs."

"Oh."

"He took one look at that ground pork—"

"Say no more."

Barkley's catastrophic reaction was understandable and, still, it was much more extreme than the tremors I had. Horrible it was. Disgusting it was. But why would it drive somebody over the edge?

Judging by Barkley, I guess the mayor had been right to keep a lid on the incident.

For myself, I was really over the collywobbles this time. I'd gotten control of my horror now. Permanently.

After all, we expect people to be medical examiners, don't we? And we respect forensic pathologists and consider them admirable professional people and receive them happily in society. We're perfectly content to go to a formal dinner and eat steak next to a guy who only a couple hours before has been up to his elbows in livers and intestines.

But having thought all this, I was suddenly hit with an idea that really did make my blood run cold.

Is it possible that Lawyer Barkley was afraid the victim was somebody he knew?

Since I had come in early and because Monday was a slow day, I was out by four. Nina asked me as I was leaving to tell her boyfriend, who was waiting for her in the parking lot, that she'd be out at five.

"Is this Gregory?" I asked.

"No, Benjamin."

By four-thirty, my brand-new windshield and I were pulling into the lot of the Cook County medical examiner's office at 2121 West Harrison.

"We aren't anywhere near done," Dr. Donald Washington said. "And I'm busy."

McCoo's note made him talk to me, but it didn't make him pleasant. The Office of the Medical Examiner of Cook County is independent of the police, and often they are at pains to show it.

"Dr. Washington, I know when the police find a body, that body comes here, to the medical examiner. When someone dies without a doctor in attendance, that body comes here. I know when the police find trace evidence, like blood, it goes to the crime lab. But who gets the evidence from the Spenser and Angelotti meat cases? What's the presumption? The material may or may not be human." I added, calculating the nature of the man, "Who's in charge of this?"

"I am. It comes here." He added, "And you've left out the hundred-and-fifty-pound metal drums of meat scraps, the drums of bones, and the drums of fat that were going to be picked up by the renderers."

"Have you found any human remains?"

116

"Of the material gathered Saturday night, no."

"You've done it all?"

"Didn't I just say we weren't finished? The mayor isn't allowing me to use the whole staff, you know. I've got *one* assistant."

"Well, what have you done so far?"

"Almost all the meat and bones from the display cases. We haven't got to the drums of scraps yet. Naturally, they're being kept refrigerated."

"But there are no human remains in all the meat from the cases you've checked? How do you know?" This was exactly what I had predicted.

"We've run antisera tests on the blood associated with the meat. It tends to leak to the bottom of the tray. Briefly, these antisera tell us whether the blood is human. Just to double-check, we run a second antiserum test to verify that it's cow, lamb, pig, and so on."

"Or chicken."

"With chickens you don't even have to bother. You can just swipe a smear on a slide. A glance through an ordinary light microscope is enough. Even *you* could do it. Avian red blood cells are nucleated. Human erythrocytes have no nuclei." He dusted his hands together. "I have to get back to work, Ms. Marsala."

"Wait. There are still more packages coming in, aren't there? From the recall notice. Meat. Bones. Who gets those?"

"We do. They are just pouring in."

"Have you tested them?"

"Just started. We're barely keeping up."

I had visions of body drawers filled with pounds and pounds of hamburger and pork sausage. How grotesque. Only, why would this be more grotesque than corpses? Actually, of course, the ME had special cold cases for body parts and wouldn't use the body drawers.

"So none of the returned merchandise so far is human?"

"No."

"What about ground meat? Could it—uh—be mixed?"

"We thought of that. We spot-check here and there in a pound, say, of ground beef. We especially check anything where the color or the coarseness of the grind varies."

"Oh. Can you identify the victim yet?"

"No."

"What about DNA matching of the bone I found?"

"You need something to match it *to*. We're working our way through it in a careful and professional manner, Ms. Marsala. I'll let Chief McCoo know when we have anything." He started to walk away.

"Wait! You must know *something* about the bone."

"Oh, that it's human, of course. But we knew that."

"What else do you know about it?"

"Ah, about thirty to forty years old, white, weight about a hundred and fifty pounds. Not particularly athletic, judging from wear and the muscle attachments."

"I see. Nothing else?"

"Exsanguinated."

"Meaning?"

"Lost a lot of blood before its owner died. And there's some osteoarthritis. I'm going to get my bone man to take a closer look at it," he added, as if there was something on his mind.

"And that's it."

"Well, we sexed it, of course."

"Sexed it?"

"Determined the sex."

"And?"

"A male, of course."

Unlike Dr. Washington, the head of the crime lab, Albert Honneker, was very gracious. This was not terribly surprising. He was in and of the Chicago Police Department, so Chief McCoo's word was law to him.

It was also his nature. Honneker was one of those pleasant, frog-shaped men, with a froggy, jolly face, large eyes, wide mobile mouth, and a little tiny nose. Honneker's face, voice, and body language all telegraphed that more than anything else he wanted everybody to be happy. You wouldn't have thought it to look at him, but he was one of the most exacting and skilled crime lab directors in the last thirty years.

"They had to bring me into the deep, dark, secret," he said, smiling broadly.

"I figured."

"I really don't think they can keep this under wraps indefinitely. I did all the work here myself, with just Chet and Phillis helping. They've been pulled off all other jobs for the time being and their samples are isolated. We aren't done yet, by the way, not by a long chalk. Ms. Marsala, I know my people don't talk. But really, this is the kind of story that wants to leak."

"Yes, you may be right."

"There is a *gargantuan* amount of stuff. Phillis Humphries is the very best there is, but she's inclined to sample everything in sight."

"Well, frankly, she had two detectives and the chief of detectives breathing down her neck."

"Right. She'd hardly want to overlook something would she?" He chuckled.

He stood up. "Come with me."

Chet Parker, the younger one of the evidence techs that had come to the scene Saturday night, was in a room next to Honneker's, fiddling with a keyboard. Images of a partial, rather fuzzy fingerprint appeared on a monitor in front of him in white against a dark blue background.

Chet was a boyish-looking person who was probably forty and looked twenty-two. He had a round face and red hair. For some reason, people with red hair always look younger than they are, at least to me. Silly, but there it is.

I said, "Hi."

He said, "How ya doing?"

Honneker said, "Tell Ms. Marsala what you're working on."

"It's okay to talk?"

"Of course. She was there. She found the bone." To me he said, "We're being *very* careful to keep this under wraps."

"Don't want the mayor on our case," Chet said. "What I'm doing is, see, that's a video camera scanning a very faint picture of friction ridges. A fingerprint. Your fingerprints evolved to make your hands better able to grab things. Hence, friction ridges. The palms and the soles of the feet have friction ridges too."

"Chet is augmenting the faintest prints. A video camera can distinguish hundreds more shades of gray than the human eye."

"Watch this." Before my eyes, the print on the screen that had been fuzzy started clarifying. "I'm basically telling it to make decisions about certain in-between shades. Eliminate some and heighten others."

"It's magic."

"No, no, it isn't," Honneker said. "It can't give you what isn't there. It just makes you see it more clearly."

Chet said, "What's a blur to you can be a hundred distinguishable shades of gray to the computer."

We tromped down a hall past several labs with staff doing bench tests of various pieces of evidence. Honneker veered left into a small, perfectly square room and there, gazing at a large box, was Phillis Humphries. On a table lay a huge pile of dirty, crumpled paper towels, maybe a hundred or so. On a stand was a large box constructed of a plastic frame and glass sides. Cords ran across the top of the box and, hanging from them like wet washing, were about fifteen crumpled, used paper towels. Over the top of the box was the hood of an exhaust fan, purring softly. There was an intense pungent chemical smell that reminded me of swimming pools.

Humphries looked away from her job for a few seconds and said, "Hi."

Honneker said, "I wanted to show Cat your chart."

"Give me a minute. I don't want these to develop too much."

"Develop like film?" I asked, seeing a camera on the bench.

"Sort of. There are iodine crystals in the dish under there." Aha. Iodine was chemically in the same family as chlorine, which was why I thought of swimming pools. Phillis pointed at the bottom of the glass box. "Iodine discolors material exposed to it. Fingerprints contain organic compounds from the skin, and they discolor very strongly. The iodine fumes in here are developing fingerprints on the paper towels."

"Neat!" I said.

"Unfortunately, iodine also develops other organic stuff, like traces of blood. Some kinds of soap. And even the folds in the towels. And these towels are really wrinkled."

"I can see that."

"They're almost ready."

"How can you tell?"

"It's really a no-brainer. I just watch until the paper itself starts to darken a little. If you let the paper get too dark, you lose contrast between the print and the paper. These are just getting close to done."

While she was watching the towels, I asked, "Do you ever use ninhydrin? I hear about it all the time."

"Oh, ninhydrin was the latest thing for a while. It is very commonly used, but it's not any better for paper towels than this. It brings up amino acids in the fingerprints. One thing ninhydrin's great for is sweaty hands. Our guy may have been sweating from head to toe, but he must've had to keep wiping his hands to get the blood off. So I doubt his fingers had sweat on them. We're looking for blood residue more than amino acids in sweat."

Checking the towels, she went on. "You can bring up the salts in sweat nicely with silver nitrate, too. If this was old paper it would be different. Salts in sweat migrate out in paper over time, but the amino acids in sweat don't blur very much. So ninhydrin's what you want for old prints. There have been cases where ninhydrin brought up fingerprints in paper that was forty years old. That's what gave it its huge rep. Big media deal. Course, our paper here is only three days old."

She peered at the towels though the glass.

She flicked a switch that increased the power of the exhaust fan from "lo" to "hi" and opened the box. The towels on their clips lifted out in one whole bunch, which she then flapped in the air. Sticking the set on a frame, she said, "Ready. I'll photograph them when I get back."

Honneker said, "Let's go."

"Phillis gridded off the floor and took one swab every twelve inches. The butcher shop is twenty by thirty feet. So she made twenty rows of thirty swabs. Six hundred swabs. She numbered them all."

"My compliments," I said.

"Then she tested them for blood. Virtually *every damn swab* tested positive for blood. Five hundred ninety-four out of six hundred."

Phillis said, "Then I tested for human blood."

"And here's what she came up with," Honneker said proudly, "when she plotted it all out."

A big graph chart displayed a grid pattern of twenty lines crossing thirty lines at right angles. At each intersection there was either an empty circle, a black dot representing blood, or a red dot representing human blood.

Also drawn on the graph were the locations of equipment—sinks, tables, storage racks, equipment cabinets, standing table saws, doors to the hall, the storage rooms, the bathroom, and the back exit.

The black dots, as Honneker had said, were just about everywhere. There were only six intersections with an empty circle, most of them back against the wall under sinks, and one behind the out-swing of the hall door. But the red dots formed a pattern. They trailed solidly across the middle of the room and were more loosely spread to and fro on the sides of this path. The floor washing had spread the human blood, I thought. They did not go to the room's corners, and the black dots did. They did not go solidly up to the hall door, although there were a couple, probably carried there on shoes. But they were dense between one of the large tables, the central sink, the knife rack, the big table saw, and the bathroom.

It was as if I were looking at the murderer in action.

"So I think we can trace his movements," Honneker said, handing me tea in a beaker. We were standing near a worktable in his office. On the table were several slides with case numbers and words like "fecal sample C-179." Honneker had two croissants right near the slides. The croissants were wrapped and the slides had cover glass, but gee. Two other beakers in his room held soil samples and one held clear glass beads. I presume he'd washed the beaker he gave me, but I wished he'd keep his specimens separate.

All the lab techs and MEs I know do this. They make no distinction between desk space for samples and desk space for lunch.

"There was no human blood in the samples from the walls."

"Interesting."

"We got a weak human blood reaction

from the center sink drain. Which is pretty good going, considering that that sink was probably in use all day Saturday."

I said, "Right. They have a reduced staff on Saturday in the butcher shop, though. Their heavy production of basics like ground beef and steak is done during the week. Especially Friday to get ready for the weekend."

"So what do they do on Saturday?"

"Specialty items. Like if a customer comes in and wants stuffed shoulder of veal. Also anything for the caterers that can't be made up ahead of time. And they replace any items that are running low."

"Huh. Well, that must be why we got a decent reaction from the saw. Maybe they didn't use it much after the killer used it."

"Which saw?"

"The band saw. The blade was positive for human blood."

"Anything else?"

"The inside upper rim of the toilet, and inside one of the garbage disposals."

"Unfortunately, what you have is trace evidence of the victim, not the killer."

"Well, it certainly confirms the location of the crime."

"Yeah, but it would be nice to know something about the killer."

"We've got just one blood type here, so that's probably not the killer either. We're taking fingerprints of all the staff."

"For elimination purposes?"

"Not necessarily. Naturally there are people you'd expect to leave their fingerprints there.

The butchers. The catering staff, I suppose. But suppose we find one of the cashiers? Or Spenser, or Angelotti? Do the owners go in there much?"

"I haven't seen them."

"And then there's the face powder."

"What face powder?"

"There was a trace of it on the floor under the front of the center sink. And none of the butchers is female."

"Just ordinary cosmetic face powder?"

"Look's like it. But we haven't been able to determine the brand. We're sending it on to the FBI lab."

✧ 13 ✧

"Cover and bake at a temperature hot enough to maintain the liquid at a gentle simmer."

"I had such a good narrative of the crime," I said to Sam, while dinner gently simmered. "Gretzka had killed his wife Sophie and disposed of her body in a way he believed to be unnoticeable."

"Well, I'm sorry, but it did look like a male femur to me, you know."

"I know. You said so at the time. What I don't

understand is, if it's not Sophie Gretzka, then where is she?"

"And where's Serge Gretzka?"

"Exactly. They found some face powder in the butcher shop, and none of the butchers is female. Do you suppose the bone is Serge's? And Sophie killed him, cut him up, and then fled? Just the same as I thought about her? Except backward, of course."

"That makes the most sense on the information you have so far. If you've got two people missing and a dead body, one of them is the body and one is the killer. Speaking of missing persons, where's Dapper?"

"Hermione came back from the wedding and picked him up. She was absolutely beside herself at the poor quality of the food at the wedding. The family had paid serious money to the caterer and got coleslaw, dried-out chicken, Jell-O, and cake mix cake. 'Perfunctory,' is what she called it when she wasn't using unquotable words."

"She would."

He was right. Hermione owned and ran Hermione's Heaven, the best restaurant in Chicago for no-nonsense eating. Lots of butter and chocolate.

Sam said, "Did she notice Dapper's ear?"

"Yeah. I felt so guilty. She said Long John Silver was an assassin."

"You do too much of that feeling guilty stuff. She should be grateful."

"Darn right."

"Long John Silver certainly looks delighted that Dapper is gone."

128

Hearing his name, LJ flew down and sat on my shoulder, very piratical. "LJ hates pets," I said.

LJ said, "Braaaaak!"

Sam said, "Dinner smells good."

"I think it's ready." From the oven I took a crock filled with ratatouille that I had bought at Spenser and Angelotti. Bruno had told me to cover the top with Parmesan and Romano cheese, put it in a crock in a low oven, and let it meld its flavors for an hour or so. "Eggplant, zucchini, tomatoes, green and red peppers, onions, garlic, a little more garlic just in case there wasn't enough, red wine, and a fragrant Ligurian olive oil. From Spenser and Angelotti."

"Yum."

I don't have a dining room table, because I don't have a dining room. When I'm alone I eat from my lap, usually on the sofa, watching television news, or my personal favorite, The Weather Channel. We sat at the kitchen table that I ordinarily used for my word processor, monitor, and printer. These items were cleverly stored on the floor.

"And polenta. With grilled mushrooms."

"Not the lasagna?"

"*No!* I mean, no."

"Did you freeze it?"

"No. Not exactly."

He looked at my face for about three seconds, then I saw awareness dawn as his eyes widened as he realized I had taken the meat lasagna in to the lab. But he didn't say another word about it. What a nice man he was.

I brought a salad out of the refrigerator and let Sam toss it, using the mild olive oil the olive oil lady had recommended, vinegar, cracked black pepper, and more garlic. I uncorked a white wine. LJ rode back and forth on my shoulder as I performed these tasks. The three of us ate in happy, companionable silence for a few minutes. LJ had two pieces of his favorite treat, a banana.

Sam said, "Disgust is a funny thing. It's a necessity for survival. Did you know, if you set out poison for rats, they 'assign,' so to speak, one or two of their members to taste it. And if they get sick or die, none of the others eat it after that."

"Smart."

"Instinctive. If you've ever eaten something you don't usually eat, and then come down with stomach flu, you probably were disgusted at the thought of that particular food, maybe for years afterward."

"Happened to me when I was a little kid. My mother had made instant butterscotch pudding. I was sick that night. Nobody else was, so it wasn't the pudding, but I refused to eat butterscotch pudding ever again. My mother was very annoyed with me."

Sam nodded, grinding a little pepper onto his salad.

He sat back and said, "The idea of cornea transplants was considered utterly disgusting when it was first introduced in England. People thought having parts of the dead put into them was an ugly idea, completely repulsive. And it is, isn't it? For a while there was even a legal prohibition against using parts of the dead. Then the medical profession and the government put on an intensive media campaign to turn public taste around. Today we'd be kind of bemused at the thought that anybody would rather be blind than have a cornea transplant. It's not considered disgusting at all. Think of the number of people who can see today, just because of cornea transplants."

"Let alone all the people who would be dead if it weren't for kidney transplants."

"Cadaver skin grafts save lives, too. But it's basically putting dead people's skin onto live people."

"You know, that feels icky to me."

"We put the horrible elements of it out of our minds. Still, I think there's real value in always, or almost always, facing up to reality. I remember to this day how confused I was when my parents told me they had to put my dog, Bognor, to sleep."

"You named your dog Bognor?"

"Yes. The problem with saying you put a dog to sleep—"

"Why Bognor?"

"Why not? You're very distractible."

"It's part of my charm."

"You wish. Listen, for about three weeks after Bognor died, I was terrified about going to sleep. Because I knew Bognor wasn't going to wake up. What if it happened to me, too?"

"Well, what should they have told you?"

"They should have said, 'Sam, Bognor has a spinal cord tumor. You know we've been giving him painkillers, but they're not enough anymore. We want to put him out of his pain. This is called euthanasia, and it means Bognor will be dead. But he won't be suffering any-more.'"

"You think you would have understood all that?"

"Most of it. The point is, I wouldn't have been given any *mis*information."

"You think human beings could live with total honesty?"

"I don't have any objection to the kind of small lie that makes somebody feel okay. Like when you tell a friend 'Nice tie' when what you would say if you were totally honest is, 'What were you *thinking*?' But we do some loony things—use a laughing cow picture to advertise a steak house! Isn't that grotesque? Isn't that almost a psychotic alienation from reality?"

"You're right that we've learned to kind of put certain things out of our minds. Like, we accept autopsies of people we love. Even though we *know* it means cutting them up. If we pictured it—yuk!"

"And funerals. We know that the dead are embalmed, and if we thought about it, we'd know it meant draining body fluids and pumping in chemicals. We even 'view the remains' without really thinking about what went on before."

I smiled. "I was driving over to the store today by a different route, from the auto glass repair shop actually, and I passed a funeral home with an advertising sign in its parking lot. It said DIGNIFIED CREMATION. What could a dignified cremation possibly be?"

"I'm picturing it now, and it's not dignified."

"Also, what's an undignified cremation? I thought, someday I'll do an article on funeral customs. I did a little cyber-search research. In Japan, cremation was illegal until 1975. It was considered disgusting. Now it's almost universal. In only twenty years, they've turned taste around."

"Maybe they ran out of extra land for cemeteries."

"I found out that in the U.S. only eight percent of the population is cremated. In Germany, the U.K., and Denmark more than half the dead are cremated."

"Did you know that in Mexico there are cemeteries where the family has to keep paying for the space and your body gets taken out if your relatives don't pay?"

"Where do they put them?"

"I don't know. But the bodies are sort of dehydrated, and they're in catacombs, so picking them up and moving them isn't really difficult."

"Embalmed like Egyptian mummies?"

"I think it's natural desiccation. But the Egyptians had a naturally drying environment, too. They added a technique of removing the organs and the brain. They removed the brain through the nose with a bronze hook. Then they preserved the body in natron— sodium carbonate and sodium chloride, ordinary salt—to desiccate it more. And then they rubbed it with unguents and put on the cloth wrapping that made them famous."

"And those beautiful sarcophagi to cover it all up."

"Speaking of cover-ups, now that there've been so many X-ray studies done of Egyptian mummies, we know that good workmanship wasn't always the case. Some mummies that look great from the outside turn out to be just a bag of bones, nicely wrapped. Sometimes the whole mummy is just a bunch of palm fronds wrapped in linen with a face painted on the front. Sometimes they skipped most of the embalming process or left out the expensive unguents, or filled the belly cavity up with whatever was handy, rocks and pieces of wood or leaves. Shortcuts to make bigger profits on the work."

I said, "Gee, there's something kind of consoling about that."

"What do you mean?"

"Well, that human nature is the same through the ages. We think that the chicanery and chiseling we see these days is some horrible effect of a strange modern loss of values. It's kind of great to know that cheap chiseling has always been with the human race."

"I guess, if you put it that way," he said.

"They probably figured nobody would want to check or even think about it. Like burial at sea," I said. "We've been taught to think of it as very romantic. But really not to *think* about it at all. Really—ugh! Fish tearing at the cloth wrapping. Shreds coming off. Flesh exposed. Then you're just—mm—lunch."

"We seem to be talking about this and eating dinner at the same time."

"I guess we're heartless. Or hungry."

"So hungry you could eat a horse? Food prejudices define people. Americans used to be disgusted that the French ate snails."

I said, "In *Dracula,* Renfield was characterized as evil just by having him eat insects. But there are parts of the world where it's considered immorally wasteful not to use insects as a source of protein."

"The sad thing is, food prejudices don't just define people, they divide people. A lot of Asians think that anyone who eats cheese is a barbarian."

"I had a great-uncle who visited his wife's family in Texas in 1957," I said. "They served him calves' brains and eggs for breakfast. He left for Chicago on the very next train, and never went back. It wasn't only that he didn't think he'd like calves' brains and eggs, or that he didn't want to eat it. It was that he couldn't stand to be in the same room with people *who ever ate it.*"

Sam laughed.

"He was narrow-minded," I said. "He should have been more open to a slightly different culture. His mind should have been more of a bridge. That's the soul of writing, isn't it? What is writing if not a bridge?"

I thought, my work as a reporter, at its best, is a bridge between people. I go out and find facts about something that many people may not know. The artistry, if I'm lucky enough to come up with any, lies in selecting the elements that are the most important and then putting them together in a way that is fair to the material, accessible, and interesting. When I'm feeling pleased with myself, it is a result of doing just that, bridging information to people, without distortion, like a window—no, not quite like a window, maybe more like a lens, collecting and focusing but maintaining clarity and truth.

Oh, well, very fancy thoughts.

"I'm pretty fed up with disgust, in case you haven't noticed," Sam said. "Yesterday I had a young mother come tearing in with her three-year-old son. You know that most of our patients are brought in by the EMTs or police vans?"

"I know." Sam's level-one trauma unit is not the same thing as an emergency room. It's much more high-tech, and mostly people don't just walk in off the streets.

"But nobody tried to stop her because the injury was obvious. She had the child wrapped in a blanket, and he was literally *bathed* in blood. We unwrapped him, and his radial artery was totally severed. He'd put his arm through a glass door."

"How awful."

"Yeah, but between the moment he was cut, and the time his mother got him to us, he had practically bled out. I was not happy. The cut itself was only two inches long. You put direct pressure on it, bring the child in, it gets stitched up, no big deal. I mean, this truly is not brain surgery."

"Yes. Well, why didn't she?"

"I asked her that. I shouldn't have, but I was angry. She said, 'Oh, I couldn't. I just can't stand blood.' Which was also why she wrapped him up. It wasn't that she thought she'd catch AIDS from the blood or anything. She just *couldn't stand blood.* She was squeamish about it. It disgusted her."

"Oh." How awful. And how stupid.

"We have a disgust mechanism for survival reasons, like the rats. It's not supposed to cause deadly peril or death."

"Did the child live?"

"Yes. No thanks to his mother. But it was a very, very close call."

After a moment, Sam said, "So why do we get so upset about this killer disposing of this body in a meat market? The possibility of cannibalism? The Melanesians called human meat *puaka balava,* long pig. A human bone isn't going to hurt us. It was the killing that was disgusting."

"We *don't* get so upset. I'm not so upset anymore. Really. I'm over it."

"You sure? You're feeling okay?"

"I'm worried about Bruno, but I don't get the shivers anymore. I'm *completely* over that."

He smiled. "Then how do you explain this?"

"This what?"

"This dinner."

"What's wrong with it?"

"Nothing. It's delicious. But it was totally vegetarian."

I looked at the damn table and my mouth

fell open. I could feel a hot red blush creep up my neck, up my chin, and over my face. "Swear to God, Sam, I never noticed."

"My point exactly."

"I never even thought about it. Today at the store, I looked at that nice sirloin steak while I was buying the other ingredients, a beautiful, aged, tender cut of beef, and I sort of walked away."

From my shoulder, Long John said, "This was the most unkindest cut of all."

Much later that evening, we sat on the sofa, Sam's arm around my waist.

"You know, Cat," he said casually, "us—together—this is very nice."

"Yes, it is."

"And rare."

"Too rare."

"We find it very difficult to coordinate our schedules."

"Right."

"If we were married, all of this would be easier."

Nervously I said, "Do you really think our schedules would suddenly coordinate better?"

He didn't take offense, but gave the comment serious thought for a few seconds.

"Well, yes. We wouldn't have to plan. We'd be in the same place a lot of the time."

"I don't know, Sam. I just don't think I can deal with this now. I'm not trying to be evasive. It's been a confusing couple of days."

In what seemed like a change of topic, he

said, "You know you could make a *huge* splash with this case. You're the only reporter who knows what's happened."

"That's true."

"What are you going to do about it?"

"Nothing. I can't hurt Bruno that way."

"I figured." He paused. "That's why I love you."

Oh, dear.

I refused to be pushed. I couldn't make my mind up, either by turning him down or accepting his offer. Instead, I jumped to my feet.

"Oh, good heavens!"

"What?"

"They pick up the trash at seven A.M., and I haven't put it out."

"Plenty of time."

"I'd just like to get it out of the way."

"I'll do it."

"No, don't bother. I need the exercise."

And the change of scene. I hurried into the kitchen and put the rest of the garbage into the bag. My back door opens—after you undo three locks—onto a flight of wooden stairs that go down to the backyard, where a cement walk holds eight square plastic cans.

I hurried down the creaking stairs. I live on the third floor, and was rounding the corner from the second floor into the last long flight, when the bag spontaneously ripped open in my hands. Next to me, a piece of the wooden railing flipped up with a *ka-chunk*!

I dove over the railing, falling ten feet to the cement areaway below.

"Bake until the meat is fork-tender."

Sam was leaning over me saying, "Tell me what day it is."

"Oh, please. That's silly. Everybody knows what day it is."

"Good. Then tell me."

I was sure I had not been knocked out, but that question was a puzzler. It certainly wasn't Sunday. I remembered Sunday happening very recently. Finally, I guessed. "Monday?"

"Hmm. All right, but I'm still worried. Can you walk upstairs?" He pulled me to a sitting position.

The garbage bag had gone over with me, and gotten between my head and the concrete. This was good, except there were coffee grounds in my ears and my forehead had been cut on an eggshell. It could have been much worse.

As we climbed the stairs, Sam said, "We should call the cops."

"Why?"

"Maybe they can find the guy."

"Here's where the shot went through the railing."

"Maybe they can trace the bullet."

"Nope." I pointed to a chip in the brick wall,

just beyond the railing. "It must have ricocheted off there. If so, it'll be a distorted mess. Even if they could find it."

I gestured along the line from the gouge in the wood to the chip in the wall and back out. If a round took a bounce at that angle, it would head out into Franklin Street under the el. Just try to find it.

"However, I will call McCoo if you insist," I said. "I think it's stupid when people keep attacks to themselves just to be macho."

I didn't mention that I had kept the smashed windshield to myself. Why arouse unwanted protective instincts?

In all, by Tuesday morning, the ME had logged in twenty-four pieces of human bone returned to the store. According to McCoo, who answered my early morning call, these were nine pieces of femur, eight pieces of tibia, seven pieces of humerus.

Dr. Washington had matched and reassembled the pieces, but not all possible parts of the six bones—left and right humerus, the upper arm bone; left and right femur, the upper leg bone; and left and right tibia, the large one of the two lower leg bones—had been found. It was interesting that no bones from any other part of the body had been returned. Only these, which were the three most massive bones in the body.

Dr. Washington was missing only a few pieces of each, maybe five or six altogether, if the size of the cuts was consistent. The bad news was, they were probably gone for good. Probably they had been used by whoever bought them and thrown out or pitched to dogs in backyards and never even thought about again.

The good news was that the bones were all from the same person; there was only one victim.

The saw marks agreed with the band saw in the butcher shop, which had been confiscated by the cops Saturday night. Saw cuts, like most tool-mark evidence, are among the easier types of evidence to be sure about. Since the days when saw marks on wood were used, rather dubiously, to convict Hauptmann of the Lindbergh baby kidnapping, tool-mark evidence has come a long way. The width of the blade produces a specific kerf, or width of cut. The set of the teeth determines the amount of ripping. And the size or coarseness of the teeth determines a smooth or rough cut. If there had been any doubt, it would even be possible to find minute fragments of metal from the blade on the bones, and match the composition of the alloy to the blade itself. This would be expensive, though, and it was easier just to keep the evidence and do the tests later if necessary.

But in this case the connection was obvious. And even though the killer had cleaned up as thoroughly as he could, inside the housing of the saw and between its teeth were traces of human blood.

And add to this the blood trail that Phillis Humphries had gridded out on her floor plan, a trail leading to the sink, the cutting table, the bathroom, and this particular saw.

Spenser and Angelotti might wish that the butcher shop was not the scene of a crime, but it clearly was.

I'm saying "scene of a crime" rather than "scene of a murder" because this didn't prove conclusively that the victim had been killed there. It was theoretically possible he had been killed elsewhere and brought there to be dismembered. But, really, that idea was far-fetched. There was too much blood on the floor for one thing. And Dr. Washington was starting to find human blood in the drums of butcher shop waste.

When I talked with McCoo on the phone, he had suggested that I stop in at the ME's office immediately. Since McCoo is Mr. Cool, "immediately" meant drop everything and move and don't even take time to ask why. When I got there, Dr. Washington was unhappy to see me and his "bone man," Dr. Ted Elsevier, was just shrugging into his coat. Asked what was new, he waved an X-ray film. He didn't explain what it was, but it certainly looked like the bone I had bought in the meat department.

"I X-rayed it. This should have been done earlier." He glanced at Dr. Washington, who looked irritably away. "See this?"

I saw "it," but I didn't know what to make of it. It looked like fuzz to me. He said, "You're aware that the inside of large bones is spongy. This is called trabecular bone. The trabecular bone in this film is coarser than normal. From the wear on the joint, there was anterolateral bowing of the femur. This was generally confirmed when I put the other pieces of bones together, even though the femur is not complete. That, together with the osteoarthritis, caused me to look closer and I found microfractures. And cortical thickening. It is paradoxical, of course. What you have here is a bone that looks enlarged and heavily calcified, but in fact is weakened."

"Which means?"

"I'm getting to that. The police say Mr. Angelotti reported that Gretzka was feeling tired. A coworker said he was having headaches. Somebody apparently told you, Ms. Marsala, that he was a man with unusually prominent temples—"

"And this means?"

"Paget's disease. Osteitis deformans. It's more common in men than women, at a rate of about three to two. Gretzka, of course, was male. It's typically a disease of Europeans, with eastern Europeans developing it slightly more than western Europeans. Gretzka is an eastern European name. It causes bone pain, stiffness, and fatigability. All of which he had."

"Is it fatal?"

"Not usually. It causes deformity, but most cases are relatively localized. What I'm saying is this. About three percent of people over forty have Paget's disease to a greater or lesser degree. Maybe one percent have it severely enough to cause significant symptoms. Gretzka had the symptoms of Paget's disease. This bone has Paget's disease. The probability is now approaching certainty. This bone is Gretzka's."

Meanwhile, on the strength of this, McCoo had gotten his detectives a warrant to search Gretzka's house. There were no dead bodies, no blood, and no Sophie Gretzka, either. There was no obvious evidence of murder plans, although the Gretzkas' personal papers would take a while to read through. They hoped to find the name of his doctor as well.

There were a lot of clothes in Mrs. Gretzka's closet, but also a large gap. Detective Torvil believed that a gap in the closet meant that some clothes were missing, but the younger detective said you got the same effect when you pushed some things aside to reach for what you wanted. Who knew? They were going to ask the neighbors if Sophie had a close friend who could tell them for sure whether clothes were missing. The next-door neighbor did not know her clothes, but said she had heard rumors the Gretzkas were separating. Sophie's parents were dead. Gretzka's mother was living, but very frail and confused.

Ominously, two lightweight suitcases stood in the front hall. The clothes in them were all men's, all of a size to fit the description of Gretzka.

In the bathroom, detectives found a comb with hair caught in the teeth that was Gretzka's dark brown color. Sophie was a blonde. Since several of the hairs still had their root, or "bulb," attached, DNA could be recovered from them. That DNA could be matched to the bone DNA.

If that was unsuccessful, there was another way to be sure whether this was Gretzka or not. Gretzka had a sister who lived in Omaha. She should share some DNA with her brother. The DNA usually tested is material from the nucleus of the cell, and inherited from both mother and father. But mitochondrial DNA, called the powerhouse of the cell, is located outside the nucleus. Since children inherit all their mitochondrial DNA from their mother, if the victim was Gretzka, the mitochondrial DNA in the bone should match the sister's exactly.

If they had to, they would even ask his elderly mother. Unfortunately, either test would take weeks.

I arrived at the store at nine-twenty, and went in through the front. McCoo had sent a detective to my apartment last night. The man had poked around, said, yup, it looked like a bullet had hit the rail and the side of the building, and nope, it wasn't likely to be found. And McCoo had told me, stay with crowds if somebody's out to get you. Big help he was. So I parked in front.

The Fern Ffolke were already in their favored spot. Inside, the olive oil lady was at work, cooking something that smelled delicious.

"Spenser and Angelotti stocks thirty-six types of olive oil," she said, over the sound of gently bubbling oil, "including many from Israel and Spain and southern California. You don't have to pay top dollar for a good, honest olive oil. It's more a matter of getting the right oil for the recipe.

"Inferior olive oils may be made from olives that have fallen on the ground. They may be overripe or bruised. The best growers suspend nets in their olive trees to catch the olives as they fall. And the very, very finest oils are made from handpicked olives."

The olive oil lady removed some fragrant, brown, crisp corn fritters from the hot oil. She said, "Drain your fritters on a wire rack."

A customer asked, "Isn't it better to drain them on paper towels?"

"You would think towels would absorb oil, and they do at first. But the fritters will quickly reabsorb oil from the paper."

I got a cup of coffee from the urn in the employees' break room and took it to the catering office. The break room is next door to the catering office, and the catering office is next door to the bakery. I pushed my chair sideways so I could see Bruno's office door from where I sat. Right now it was open, which meant that he wasn't in, and I had seen no one at his desk when I came down the hall. My purpose was to catch him and slip inside when no one was watching so I could talk with him unnoticed by the other employees.

I took a sip of the coffee. Not bad. Even McCoo would have to admit this was good stuff. Bruno told me, when I was here months ago doing the interview for the *Chicago Today* article, that you couldn't expect employees to care about the food they sold if you gave them junk to eat and drink. The Spenser and Angelotti bakery supplied the break room with fresh cookies daily, and they were good, too. But what was really interesting about the store was that Bruno required the master baker, Nicholas Lane, to put a little written discussion next to them. Some days it was the ethnic heritage of the cookie. Some days it was instruction on cookery.

Today's treat was:

RITA RAK'S BUTTER COOKIES

1 lb. butter
1 cup sugar
2 egg yolks
1 tsp. vanilla
4 cups flour

Cream butter and sugar. Add egg yolks and vanilla. Gradually add flour. Roll out and cut with cookie cutter or put through a sturdy cookie press. Bake at 350 degrees about 10 to 12 minutes.

Deceptively simple, this cookie is simply delicious. It can be varied by adding grated lemon peel or orange peel, but you really don't need to gild this lily. Because it is a stiff dough, it can be formed into wreaths or other shapes for holidays.

When making cookies such as chocolate chip, variations in certain ingredients can tailor your results. Butter makes a cookie

dough spread out as it cooks. Half short-
ening and half butter makes a cookie that
holds its shape. Cake flour produces a
lighter, puffier cookie, while all-purpose
or bread flour will make a darker, flatter
cookie. Substituting corn syrup for some
of the sugar makes a browner cookie.

—NICHOLAS LANE

Bruno Angelotti was educating his employees
every minute.

He had told me, "I want a staff that can
answer the customer's questions. We're not
like other supermarkets."

I had just taken a catering call, and then a
third and fourth sip of my coffee, when Paul-
Michel Cartier came in, carrying a sheaf of
papers.

"I have this new order," I said.

"And what would it be?"

"Well, it's a wedding at a church on the north
side. Two hundred guests. The reception is in
the church basement. The bride's mother
says the space has only a two-burner stove,
an oven, and a small refrigerator."

"Could be worse. One of us will have to go
look."

"But she was kind of—defensive. She told
me several times that the words 'church basement' didn't really describe it. She said the
basement, and she sounded pained when she
used the word 'basement,' was, as she put it,
'a very elegant venue, actually,' with walnut
paneling and carpet."

He said, "I see. So they will want elegant

149

foods. Fussy, pretty foods. Salads with edible flowers on them. Trout stuffed with crab. An exotic vegetable. Possibly they would find braised endive to be exotic. And a very traditional cake, white, lots of frosting flowers, maybe candied violets, and seven or eight tiers."

"Well, I guess."

"You sound doubtful. Ms. Marsala, we may have ideas about what we would have at our own parties, but we have to be sensitive to the feelings of our customers. However foolish."

"Oh, well. Yes, of course."

"I'm going to talk with Lane about the madeleines for Tiffany's. I'll be back." He strutted out of the office with his head high.

At about that same moment, I saw Bruno walking down the hall to his office. Dack passed by a few seconds later. He was pushing a wheeled cart filled with large roasts for the meat case. I took one more sip of coffee to give him time to pass, jumped up, and peered around the door. The double doors to the sales floor flapped closed behind Dack. The corridor was unoccupied.

I knocked on Bruno's door.

"Come in."

He was studying a dozen or so colorful advertising flyers from food producers. One showed a tree full of tangerines. Another three-fold sheet had glossy color pictures of a bowl of salted pecans, a luscious pile of pecan pralines, and a view of a pecan plantation or field or orchard or whatever you call it when it's nut trees.

Bruno said, "Sit down. How does your investigation go?"

"I'm not sure. You've heard about the returned bones?"

"Yes. Twenty-four with some missing."

"My guess is the rest won't be returned."

"The medical examiner called me an hour ago." His voice was much sadder and his face older than the Bruno I had met six months earlier.

"What did he say?"

"They've found small human bones in the drums of waste bones."

"But nothing else?"

"They say nothing else. Just bones."

"Bruno, two dozen or so extra bones, not in inventory, went into the meat case between Friday night and Saturday morning. Why didn't anybody notice the discrepancy?"

"Why would they? The butchers and their assistants put meat out, but they don't know how much is sold."

"Well, who tells them to produce more of something, more ground beef, for instance?"

"Henry or I or the senior butcher will check the cases. Every hour or so. But it isn't set up so any one of us keeps exact count. If the butchers look and see only ten packages of hamburger, they know they need to grind more or get it out of the cold room and fill the case."

"Well, would the cash register results tell you there were more bones being sold than was right?"

"The cash registers do record the quantity

of items sold and check for proper pricing, but they don't know exactly how many packages of each type of meat the store is supposed to have. That is, of the meat we cut here. Beef isn't a standardized product. We know how many six-packs of Coke we have, but one side of beef may give more good steak, another more ground beef. The meat may be cut up differently from one carcass to another."

"Why?"

"Well, you know we want to sell the best. If the butcher decides that this particular side looks tougher than most, he will choose to make more of it into ground beef. Or pot roast. Or stew. Plus, people use more steaks in the summer and more roasts in the winter. That's why we have master butchers, and why we buy whole sides. Shippers can't put anything over on us. We also discard more than other stores."

"It's a lot more work."

"And more expensive. And safer. We grind our own hamburger meat. Most people think all stores grind their own hamburger, but they don't. They buy meat coarse ground in ten-pound units called 'chubs.' Then they regrind it. But that chub can contain beef from a hundred cows, mixed together. That means if there's contamination, if one cow was sick or one carcass contaminated, beef from hundreds of other cows gets contaminated, too. And there's pork in it sometimes, and scraps of all kinds of meat. And the beef can come from four or five other countries besides the U.S. If there's some bacteria in it, you can't even trace back to the source. Our ground beef is wonderful, like real French *bifteck haché*. Many of our customers come here just for the ground beef. It is just so ironic that we would have this horrible problem."

"Okay. But your butchers still must have a close idea of how much they're producing."

"Most of the time the senior butcher doesn't stock the cases himself. He's a highly paid professional. He cuts, he trims, he judges quality. Various helpers usually stock the cases. The label generator keeps track of how much is being packaged."

"It sounds like a loophole in your cost accounting."

"We want to sell the very best. We look at the side of beef and see how good it is. Like I tell you, we decide what cuts to make when we see it. If we let somebody else do that for us, we lose quality control." He added that constant Spenser and Angelotti refrain, "We're just not like other stores."

"You know those packages of human bones were dated Saturday."

"Yes."

"But there's no time of day on the package. McCoo thinks the murder happened about one A.M. Saturday morning. Is it possible the murder took place earlier?"

"The dates advance automatically at midnight."

"Could somebody fudge the dates? Commit the murder Friday or even Thursday, for instance, set the package date to Saturday, then set it back to Friday or Thursday before he left?"

153

"Impossible. The dates can't be set in the butcher shop. They're set from Henry's office. There is a motion detector in the hall, so the killer could not get to the office."

"I see. Let me change the subject. Was Serge Gretzka worried about anything when you talked with him last? Could somebody have been threatening him?"

"Threatening him? I cannot imagine such a thing. He was a nice man. I mean he *is* a nice man. Oh, dear! When will I know for sure?"

"Soon, I think." I was sure now.

"As to whether he was worried, I think not. But he didn't feel well."

"You told me he was tired."

"And having headaches. I think a vacation will help him. That is, of course—oh, dear."

❖ 15 ❖

"Chop parsley, garlic, and lemon peel. Mix one part of garlic and one part of lemon peel to three parts of parsley to make a *gremolata*."

I left Bruno to go on with his ordering.

Unfortunately, despite what he said, the dates on the packages *could* have been rigged. But only by Henry Spenser or Bruno Angelotti.

The controls were in Spenser's office. Only they knew the code.

Nobody could get into the marketing area or the office hall without setting off the alarm system. Unless they were one of the people who each night *set* the alarm system. Bruno or Henry.

And either of them could have waited to set the alarm until after the killing and dismembering was finished.

I found Tim Savage, the cop, interviewing one of the cashiers in a discreet corner of the coffee bar. That's Tim for you; he'd decided that comfortable chairs and a constant supply of coffee would contribute significantly to his investigative acuity. While he finished with the cashier I pretended to study a display of several kinds of biscotti. Why anybody would want to eat vanilla or lemon biscotti, I don't know. If you can't have cocoa-almond biscotti dipped in dark chocolate, you might as well go hungry.

Tim beckoned me over when the cashier had left. I said, "Pretend you're interviewing me."

"Sure. Sit down."

"Are you trying to find out where any of these people were last night when I got shot at?"

"Yeah, of course. I got the directive from McCoo."

"I don't suppose any of them admit to being outside my apartment at eleven P.M."

"No. But I can't ask that. I just get to ask where they were. A lot of them claim to have been with somebody else. Most of them were perfectly free to shoot you."

155

"Spiffy."

"Not Nina Timko. She was with some guy named—"

"Gregory? Benjamin?"

"Cassius."

"Oh."

"Hey, I have a secret," he said. "Come with me. I just found the best place in the store."

"For what?"

"The best place to be."

"I can't go anywhere with you. People aren't supposed to know that I know you, except you get to ask questions."

"Well, then call me 'officer.' Act formal. Come on."

He walked into the bakery, me trailing along. Whenever we passed staff people, I'd say, "Where are we going, Officer?" I don't know whether we fooled them or not.

Nicholas Lane had apparently gone on break; the pastry hunk was not in sight. At one side of the bakery, which right now smelled of rum cake, Tim pointed to a rack. It was full of cakes, pies, breads, and cookies. "Look at that."

"Yes. So?"

"You can eat any of this. Just pick something."

"You can't just take these."

"Yes, you can. They're rejects. They can't put 'em on the sales floor because they're flawed."

"Oh."

"I had a pecan pie for lunch. A *whole pie.*

And all that was wrong with it was, when somebody was taking it out of the oven, it slid sideways and got wrinkled."

Back at my desk, I put the plate of three luscious chocolate éclairs next to my coffee cup. I tasted one. Mmm-mmm. Great! The only reason they'd been rejected was that their frosting was too runny.

Deliciously, chocolate-runny. Creamy vanilla custard-center goodness. I drank some coffee, and ate more chocolate éclair.

Quite suddenly, perspiration sprang out on my forehead. What was happening? A horrible, hollow sensation started in my stomach. I began to sweat all over my body. Then came the nausea. I swallowed, and swallowed, and swallowed again. I felt cold and sick.

I jumped up and ran out of the catering office, past the door to the bakery and the deli/catering kitchen, trying not to be sick in the hall. I was so embarrassed.

Into the bathroom. Thank God! I felt horrible. In seconds, I was sick, but I made it to the toilet in time. Good Lord, what had happened?

I stood reeling, dizzy in the head, cold all over. Then I was sick again. And again.

And then it was over.

I waited, puzzled, thinking if I had the flu or food poisoning, it wasn't going to be as easy as all that. But I certainly felt better. Really, not bad at all. This was *not* normal.

I went to the sink and washed my face and

rinsed my mouth. Still okay. Pacing back and forth a minute or two didn't produce any yucky symptoms, either.

Well, all right. Good.

I walked back to the catering office, shaken, wondering what that was all about. When I got to my desk, my eyes fell on the coffee and the remaining éclair.

Poison?

Was it possible?

I hurried out through the doors into the store, where I grabbed a jar of baby food off the shelf. The larger jar for toddlers.

Back to the bathroom. I poured the contents, vegetable-beef stew, into a toilet and flushed it away. I rinsed the jar several times at the sink, then returned to the catering office.

Into the jar, I poured most of the remaining coffee. I wrapped the éclair in paper. I wandered casually into the bakery carrying the jar and the éclair and pulled a brown bag from the supplies shelf. The jar and the éclair went into the bag.

Out in the Coffee Café, Detective Tim Savage was about to start questioning one of the maintenance men. I slipped in first.

I said quietly, "Tim. Can you have these tested for poison?"

He goggled at me. Then, glancing around and realizing that there were a lot of people, if not within earshot then close to it, he said, "Oh, of course, Ms. Marsala. It will be delicious for my lunch. And thank the baker, Mr. Lane, for me."

For several minutes I considered Nicholas Lane. I wanted to go and accuse him of poisoning me. But the éclairs really weren't a likely source of poison. At least, not of selective poison aimed at me. I'd randomly picked three out of a batch of two dozen rejects that had the runny chocolate frosting.

Although custard was a famous source of food poisoning—innocent food poisoning—it was hard for me to believe that a bakery as fastidious as Spenser and Angelotti's would leave custard lying around at room temperature long enough to develop salmonella or whatever bacteria egg custard brewed up. Plus, I thought bakeries had gone over to a puddinglike custard made of cornstarch and milk and flavorings, precisely so that even if the customer didn't refrigerate the baked goods right away, nobody would get deathly sick. And besides, food poisoning takes hours to come on, not minutes. But chemical poisoning was fast.

Sabotage?

Suddenly worried, I sneaked over to Tim Savage, hoping to talk with him. He had eaten half of an éclair, and as I watched he popped the final piece into his mouth in one bite. Now I felt guilty. I should have had the sense to tell him not to eat any of them until he got the stuff tested.

It would be cruel to scare him now. Plus, I really thought it was the coffee that had made me sick, not the éclair. And since my symptoms had come on in less than two minutes, I could just keep an eye on him for a little while.

He keyed his radio, got a response from the dispatcher, and spoke.

While I waited, the olive oil lady demonstrated her wares.

"You will see on this map of Italy the shaded areas where olive oil is the principal cooking fat. In the other provinces, butter is used. Except for this small coastal area around Genoa, overlooking the Ligurian Sea, the olive oil provinces are mainly the southern part of Italy, down the back of the boot and into Sicily. Abruzzi, Molise, Campania, Basilicata, Apulia, Calabria, the island of Sardinia, and Sicily. It is said in the south that it is less expensive to keep an olive tree than keep a cow for butter. Interestingly, most of the olive oil sections of Italy also use tubular-shaped pasta, while the places that use butter traditionally eat flat pasta."

Even as I watched Savage, a patrol cop came in. Savage handed him a bag—my bag I supposed, but now covered with a plastic outer wrapping. Savage may look rumply, but he is clever and subtle.

And he wasn't sick. Which confirmed my suspicions.

I had taken several sips of coffee, and then gone out and left the coffee sitting in the office on a desk known to be mine. I had talked with Bruno for at least ten minutes, leaving the catering office door open and the coffee unguarded. Then I had meandered my way over to Tim Savage, waited while he finished an interview, and then had gone with him to the bakery. Easily fifteen minutes. Maybe half an hour all told.

Plenty of time for almost anybody to come down the hall and poison the coffee.

Good God, right now I could be dead.

✧ 16 ✧

"Remove the bubbling casserole from the oven and turn the heat up to 450 degrees."

Why poison *me*? What do I know? Nothing! If only I did know who the killer was, I could tell somebody and get out from under. But I can't. I could walk away from it all. Chicken out? No thanks.

Maybe somebody doesn't want me at Spenser and Angelotti's. But why? Do they think I'm going to find out something that will point to the killer? That's possible. But why me? Why not the police?

Well, maybe they would attack Tim too, if they could, but maybe that's just too dangerous. And, of course, there's always another police officer where that one came from. There's only one of me.

Or the killer thinks that because I'm here as an apparently innocent civilian, I will find out something the police can't. Which means the killer has figured out that Spenser and Angelotti have asked me to be here.

Unless the killer is Henry Spenser or Bruno Angelotti.

Well, all right. Who could have access to my coffee cup?

Damn near everybody. Henry Spenser. Bruno Angelotti. Nina Timko came into the office a lot on catering errands, even though as chef she spent most of her time in the kitchens. But why would she care what I was doing? She didn't have any motive to kill Gretzka. Paul-Michel Cartier, the assistant catering manager, had easiest access of all, because he worked in the same office. And he had a motive. The butcher, Dack, was just a couple of doors away, but had no motive that I knew of. Nicholas Lane was right next door in the bakery and had flirted with the mysteriously missing Sophie.

Anybody coming into the hall to go to the staff lounge would walk right past the catering office where my desk was. Cashiers, maintenance men, delivery people. Anybody could have seen me at that desk in past days, and could have noticed the fact that my jacket was on the chair in front of the desk.

There was a bathroom in the butcher shop as well as the one in the hall, but there were no rules I knew of that the butchers had to use that one.

Even the Fern Ffolke came into the store occasionally to use the public washroom. It was in the public part of the store, of course, but this wasn't Fort Knox; there were no security guards keeping watch on the back end of the store. They might slip by unnoticed. It would be a matter of luck, though. On the whole, I thought there was too much traffic in the hall for them to chance it.

Noon. There was nothing I could do about the "poison" until we got results of the testing on the coffee and éclair. And that could be hours at the very least.

Relieved that Tim Savage seemed perfectly well, I started back toward the catering office. Sounds at the front of the store caught my attention.

When I turned around, I saw a TV news crew swarming through the front doors. Nothing else looks like these guys. When they really want to do it right, in addition to the camera with its built-in light, they bring extra camera operators, portable lights, a couple of guys to move stuff, and at least one on-camera reporter. Also, of course, one or two guys to head off grandstanders—those civilians you so often see behind the reporter, waving their hands and making faces.

One of the cashiers picked up the pager and called frantically, "Mr. Spenser, Mr. Angelotti!

To the cashiers' desk please. Mr. Spenser, Mr. Angelotti!"

"So, Miss Beattie, you didn't know there were human remains being sold in the meat case?"

Pam Beattie, a nineteen-year-old cashier and possibly the tiniest person in the store, froze like a rabbit in the lights. Her wispy blonde hair danced around her face as she shook her head.

The reporter, Bill Etheridge, said, "Did you know there was a problem? Surely you had heard about the recall of meat products." Etheridge fixed her with a boyish stare. He was young, very aggressive, and said to be from a wealthy North Shore family. A hungry reporter.

"I thought that was—uh—not—wasn't very important." Pam backed away as she talked, but she couldn't go far. Etheridge had cleverly cornered her up against the side of the checkout stand, with the whole store as a backdrop behind her.

"*What the hell is this?*" Henry Spenser yelled, barreling through the clump of amazed customers who were watching the videotaping.

"I'm Bill Etheridge from Channel—"

"I know who you are! I said, what the hell is this?"

"Are you Mr. Spenser?"

"Yes. Now either you tell me what you want or I'll call the police!"

I was thinking, you won't have to call far;

there's one in the coffee bar. But of course Spenser wouldn't want them to know that.

"Mr. Spenser. We have been informed that parts of a deceased human being were being sold out of your store as food. We want to know whether—"

"Out! *Out! Out! Out!*" The cameras were rolling while he yelled.

"Mr. Spenser—"

"This is private property. Move!"

"Sir, this is a public place."

"Merchandising establishments invite the public in for a specific purpose, legally speaking. They aren't public buildings in the sense that the Cook County courts are public. I order you to leave immediately."

He said, "Sir! Don't you think you need to explain?"

But the older man with him whispered something in Etheridge's ear. He showed some confusion and was starting to turn to argue with the man when Bruno Angelotti spoke up.

Bruno's face was drawn and gray. His eyes were like a man in great pain. "I will explain what has happened. You will find you have a more accurate picture if I tell you myself. No, no, Henry," he said, as Spenser grabbed his arm. "They will only hear inflated rumors if we don't clarify."

He said to Etheridge. "Let me tell you what we know."

As he talked, a couple of the customers quietly set packages of meat down on the checkout belt and walked away, out the front doors.

We were huddled in the staff lounge—Bruno, Henry Spenser, Tim Savage, and me. Savage had gone out for a portable television set. He plugged it in and turned it on.

Etheridge was doing a "live remote" from the front of the store. There were five seconds—which seem like five minutes in TV time—of Henry screaming, "Out! Out! Out!" Then Etheridge spoke, saying, "Mr. Bruno Angelotti confirmed exclusively to this reporter that two dozen pieces of human bones were sold at Chicago's premier market, Spenser and Angelotti—"

Bruno said, "Oh, my God."

Spenser said, "Well, it's your fault! You talked to them." His face was red with anger.

"Henry, you shouldn't have yelled at them."

"You should have stonewalled them. We had every legal right to throw them out."

I said, "Oh, give it a rest, you two. Bruno's right. Once the cat is out of the bag with the media, that's it, that's all she wrote. There's a hundred ways they can confirm it once they know where to look."

"Did *you* tell them?" Spenser demanded, looking as if he loathed me.

"Please! You were afraid I'd use it for a scoop. It's no scoop if it comes out of some other reporter's mouth on the noon news."

That sort of shut him up. Then I said, "Anyway, this isn't the worst of it."

"Oh?"

"They all watch each other. I give it twenty minutes before Channels Two, Five, Seven, Nine, and Thirty-two arrive, along with the *Tribune* and the *Sun-Times*. And the *Southtown Economist* and the *Reader* and thirty or forty smaller papers. And every radio station within thirty miles."

I was wrong. It was much worse. Every reporter in town was in the parking lot or in the store by one P.M. We had Harry Porterfield and Jim Rosenfield, both, from Channel 7 and John Davis from Channel 2. The *Trib* had sent two reporters, their muckraker journalist, Boyce Kanner, plus their science reporter. The *Sun-Times* sent two also—their muckraker journalist and their *food editor*! The other news channels, 5, 9, and 32, sent one person apiece, by which I mean one reporter. That didn't count the support staff—cameraman, assistants, and so forth.

Neither Spenser nor Angelotti kept a personal secretary to answer phone calls. A young woman named Beth, who usually answered telephone inquiries, was pressed into service. Spenser told her to slam the phone down when the media called. Angelotti said, no, be nice, but tell them the event is over and there's nothing more to talk about.

By mid-afternoon Beth was frazzled and bedazzled at the same time. She'd talked with Katie Couric for the *Today Show*, Ed Bradley from CBS's *60 Minutes*, Barbara Walters for *20/20*, Stone Phillips for *Date-*

line NBC, Jane Pauley also for *Dateline NBC*, Maria Shriver for *48 Hours*, Diane Sawyer for *Prime Time Live*. Beth was ready to float to the ceiling with the thrill of it all, and yet she couldn't admit to her excitement, because Spenser and Angelotti were in terrible trouble.

"Beth," I said, "I can't believe people like that actually make their own phone calls."

"Well, not the first call. But when I told the first person that we didn't have anything to say, they had the *anchors* call back."

The *Enquirer* and *Star* offered serious money. Spenser said, snarling, "If things go on this way, we'll probably need it."

He had a point. The store was full of people, but the cash registers weren't ringing. Or to be more up-to-date, the bar code scanners weren't scanning. There were few food buyers in the place.

Oh, not zero. When people are used to shopping in a specific supermarket, they tend to keep on going there. But the media bodies outnumbered them by a lot. And the media were frustrated. With Spenser and Angelotti hiding in their offices, the reporters could only talk with the cashiers, who knew they weren't supposed to say anything. Spenser had given up demanding the reporters get out, but he ordered Tim Savage to call the local district cops in to protect the stock. I think Savage had already called for help before he was ordered to, because I didn't see him key

168

his radio and within a couple of minutes uniformed cops were in the parking lot.

At four o'clock, we saw McCoo on the Channel 7 "evening" news.

He said, "There were twenty-five pieces of human bones found, all from the same victim. This victim has been tentatively identified as Mr. Serge Gretzka, catering manager at the store. There were no human remains found in the meat being sold at Spenser and Angelotti. Nor in any of the returned meat or meat products."

The reporter for the *Trib*, Boyce Kanner said, "Yes, Chief. But why should we believe you?"

McCoo's face became stony. He always had a hard time suffering fools gladly, but he kept his voice calm and said, "Because I have never, in all the years I have been a member of the Chicago Police Department, ever lied to the press."

There was a moment of silence. Then two reporters actually booed Kanner. Boyce Kanner had the grace to look abashed.

"The city moved expeditiously to recall the products," the mayor told all major news channels live, half an hour later. "Our concern was to get any potential—ah—material back from the public and, second, to do this without panicking the public. I think we succeeded very well."

The city, though, was angry at the mayor. The "man in the street" was interviewed for the news, and the man in the street thought he should have been told. He had a right to know things like this. The people of the city weren't children. As one woman put it, "The mayor's action didn't protect anybody from anything. It was just plain, old-fashioned paternalism, and I loathe paternalism."

The mayor had looked calm on television. According to McCoo, in private he was absolutely, jaw-clenching, vein-popping, carpet-chewing, nails-spitting furious. "I'm leaving for the conference of mayors in Atlanta *tomorrow morning!*" he screamed, while the superintendent of police, the medical examiner, and McCoo stood rigid, absorbing his fury. "They'll be making jokes about Chicago. I'll be humiliated! I want you to find whoever leaked this! And when you find him, *shoot him!*"

The Fern Ffolke in front of the store disappeared for about an hour. When they returned, they were holding a long white banner with red letters: SEE HOW IT FEELS!

Just before I left my office, a call came in. It was the woman who wanted an elegant wedding reception for two hundred guests for her daughter in the basement of their north side church.

"Cancel it," she said.

170

✧ 17 ✧

"Transfer the bones carefully to an ovenproof dish, using tongs or a large spoon in order not to lose any meat or the marrow from the bones."

It was wonderful to be home in my own apartment, quiet, no reporters, no tension. I had been cautious on my way from the store to the car and from the car to my door. Nobody had attacked me.

The apartment was just as I had left it. No one had broken in. I never set any of those corny hair-in-the-doorjamb warning things to let me know if I've had an intruder. If a stranger came in here while I was gone, there would be feathers all over from a frantic, angry, hopping-mad African gray parrot.

I composed a small plate of leftovers for dinner and ate it lying in a tub of hot water, one of my favorite ways to unwind. And this was definitely a time to try seriously to relax. Bruno was in such deep distress that I had boldly called his wife at home and asked her to come and get him. Poor man. It was his whole life's work that was being trashed.

Maybe in a few days, if the furor died down, I could help him more substantially. I could write an article on where he came from, what part of Italy, what the traditional dishes were there, and how he translated some of them to the American marketplace and American ingredients. Vegetarian dishes, maybe. Maybe he could put this all behind him.

And yet, if I'm thinking vegetarian dishes, doesn't that suggest that the impact, the utter revulsion, the disgust on the part of the whole city has been equally strong?

Sam had been talking about disgust, and how counterproductive disgust could be. Disgust? There was a joke about a vulture who had been out all day and came back in the evening, looking sick. His wife said to him, "What's the matter?"

"Oh, I feel awful," he said. "I think I must have eaten something fresh."

And then there was the story of the cockroach who came home to his happy nest in the garbage can after a big day of scavenging. "You should have seen one of the places I was in today, dear," he says.

"Oh, what was it?" she says.

"Well, it was this kitchen. White tile, spotless sinks, the white refrigerator all scrubbed so it gleams—"

"Stop!" she says. "Not while I'm eating!"

Disgust really is in the eye of the beholder.

After all, suppose you're cooking onion soup made of beef broth and white wine, with cheese on top. What've you got? Boiled down roots, boiled pieces of cow, rotten grapes, and spoiled milk.

The disagreement between Henry Spenser, wanting antiseptic-looking food in square packages, and Bruno Angelotti, wanting as much of it fresh in its original state as possible, began to appear as a fundamental difference in philosophy.

The more you think about this, the more you wonder about some of your own food dislikes.

I got out of the tub, much more relaxed. Getting wet and then dry again resets your emotional thermostat. You reboot.

So let's acknowledge that the victim is Serge Gretzka, not his wife. That's all very well and good, but then where is Sophie Gretzka? She's not in Panama City. And she's not at home. Could she have been killed, too? Possibly the motive for all this is personal to the Gretzkas. Could we all be wrong in thinking that the murder was connected to Spenser and Angelotti?

Maybe somebody hated the Gretzkas. Maybe the Gretzkas were into an illegal activity, like drug distribution, that got them killed. Maybe they were gamblers and couldn't pay. I'd have to ask McCoo whether he had checked their bank account, but he would certainly answer, "Been there. Done that. Been in this business some time already." Or simply, "Cat, please!"

I cleaned up my kitchen. McCoo said be careful about taking out the garbage, but what are you going to do with garbage? Just let it ferment? I may be a casual housekeeper, but I'm not like Mr. and Mrs. Cockroach. You have to take the garbage out.

I took it out, looking all around. Nobody shot at me.

Back in my apartment, I faced the fact that I'd done everything I could think up to put off thinking about what I really should think about. Okay, Marsala, what are you going to do about Sam?

My mother wants me to settle down. She is one of those people to whom "settling down" is life's ultimate goal. We ought to be limpets. Or reef coral.

Sam is a sweetheart, and I don't say that condescendingly. He is a big, gangly, lovable kind of guy. He is easygoing in the sense that he lets people be themselves. He doesn't expect everybody to be the same and, unlike a lot of doctors I've known, he doesn't want to order you around, either.

And yet, in his work, he is decisive. You really can't be a trauma surgeon and be riddled with doubts, waiting around for somebody to tell you what to do. I respect Sam a lot. He has opinions but is willing to rethink them. He is flexible. He isn't predictable like my other longtime friend, good, solid John, who was a fine person, but not for me.

Sam is sane. It sounds like such a small thing, but when you've grown up with a mother like mine, moody and unpredictable, with unmotivated anxiety storms, there's nothing so attractive as a person who is *always the same person*.

But listing a person's good points is a distancing process. *Get a grip, Marsala.*

Am I attracted to him? Yes. I already know that. He knows it, too.

Sam is lovable. Well, we're getting closer to

what we're trying not to get closer to, aren't we? Do I love him?

Oh, for heaven's sake. Yes.

I flicked on the television, happy that the late news broadcasts were over and I wouldn't be exposed to more about Bruno Angelotti's humiliation. I was just in time to hear Jay Leno say, "You know about the pieces of a murder victim found in a meat case in a Chicago supermarket?"

Everybody chuckled uneasily.

"Gives a new meaning to the term 'rump roast.' "

They laughed.

"Or, heaven forbid, bratwurst."

They roared.

"But then, it's a fine thing to serve humanity."

Time for bed. What a day. I put Long John Silver in his cage, and just before the cover went over him, I said, "Do we want to get married, LJ? Think about it for me, will you?"

✦ 18 ✦

"Bake the veal bones in the hot oven for five to ten minutes until they are beautifully browned, but do not let them burn."

The store was a tomb Wednesday morning. Bad choice of words, maybe. There were few shoppers.

I had walked up to the front of the store, but stopped outside the doors. There was a mob of reporters eight or ten deep, plus white vans from the TV channels angled in around them, with their satellite guns on top. Several had cameramen on top as well, trying to shoot into the store through the windows from the higher vantage point.

The *Enquirer* and *Star* had sent reporters. Isn't that nice?

The Fern Ffolke were mobbed. Cameras were rolling as they told their story. This certainly was a bonanza for them. With nobody from Spenser and Angelotti giving interviews, and the police now keeping reporters out of the store, the Fern Ffolke were the most interesting thing around and getting a million dollars' worth of publicity. I must say, they were handling it with grace. They simply repeated their message, without gloating.

I went to the back and rang the back door buzzer.

"Who's there?"

"Cat Marsala."

"Oh." There was the sound of a bolt pulling back. This was new.

Paul-Michel let me in.

"Why did you bother to come?"

This guy needed some lessons in dealing with his colleagues.

"Why not?"

"Well, there's no business."

"Maybe I can help some way."

"I doubt it."

"Thanks."

I wandered into the store. From the center aisle I could see Henry Spenser and one of the store janitors, installing a banner above the deli case. Henry was gesturing to the man that the left side of the banner had to go higher.

It read: TODAY ONLY EVERY DELI ITEM HALF OFF.

Rather than embarrass him by watching, I turned down the aisle toward the cheese and past the coffee bar. The olive oil lady was there again today, with a small toaster oven. I had considered her a bit of a joke with her unwavering cheer and her little checked apron. But now there was just one customer sitting in front of her, listening. She seemed quite heroic, carrying on no matter what.

She said, every bit as pleasantly as if the chairs were full of people, "The world's finest olive oils are said by most experts to come from

Lucca, in Tuscany, which is actually north of the principal olive oil regions. But some believe the best oils are from the Sassari region on the island of Sardinia.

"Olive trees, like grapes for wine, produce the best quality in rocky, rather infertile, soil.

"Today we are using a delicate olive oil to make two lovely Italian dishes, *funghi arrostiti,* mushrooms brushed with olive oil, parsley, and garlic, and *bruschetta,* which the Umbrians in central Italy make with new, fresh, light oil.

"Olives are pressed in late summer and early fall. The crushing stones are traditionally granite. Once the olives are crushed, they are spread out on hempen mats, stacked mat upon mat, and then pressed."

A man passed behind her, pushing a shopping cart. I swear he was a reporter, even though he had a six-pack of 7-Up and a loaf of French bread in the cart. He said to her, "Do you use a light or dark olive oil to fry people?"

I gasped. But she carried on as if nothing had happened. At most her chin lifted slightly. I walked past her to go into the coffee bar, but really to smile at her encouragingly. As I turned back, I saw that the sole "audience" to whom she was lecturing was one of the cashiers.

The cheeses were a trip around the world without even moving your feet. Pecorino from Rome, all salty and robust. Goat cheese from Australia. Creamy, soft mascarpone. P'tit basque made of sheep's milk. Roquefort, and brie. French chaumont from the Champagne region, imported only from November to May. Reblochon, from the milk of ewes. The Swiss cheese Emmentaler and its French cousin, Gruyère. Dutch Edam, Leyden, and Gouda. Manchego from Spain. From England, double Devon cream, double Gloucester, and blue-veined Stilton. Cheeses blended with truffles or peppercorns, with pesto or sun-dried tomatoes. Scamorze, mozzarella, and fresh ricotta, fat little balls of bocconcini marinated in olive oil. Kauna from Lithuania.

Henry Spenser was in the dairy department. The janitor had gone away. Coming up next to Spenser, I said, "I'm sorry about all your trouble." Now I saw that he'd been placing a sign in the cold case.

"Look at this! The milk'll spoil in a few days. What am I supposed to do with it?" he grumbled. "I can cut down the next orders, but people want to buy milk with expiration dates several days in the future."

"Donate some perishables to a couple of the shelters that feed the homeless."

"Say!" he said, looking at me as if maybe I wasn't total poison, "That's really not a bad idea. I can tell the media about it. Make us look good and help them forget about the you-know-what."

"I think if we can find the killer, everybody will forget about the you-know-what."

"Christ, are you stupid!"

"Huh?"

"Oh, what difference does it make now?"

He stomped away. The sign he had been placing was TODAY ONLY—MEAT AND DAIRY PRODUCTS HALF OFF MARKED PRICE.

And I finally reached Tim Savage, who with a tech was fingerprinting "for elimination purposes," as they put it to the staff members who had been off the last two days and therefore unavailable. Now that all the staff knew somebody had been killed here, and therefore the situation was really serious, half of them were more cooperative and half were more defensive. He was also completing time sheets on where everybody had been at a variety of crucial times, not just late Friday night through early Saturday morning, but also where people were when I was attacked. Some of the people were alibiless all of the time, all of the people were alibiless some of the time, and anybody could hire somebody. So where were we?

He saw me coming.

"Ipecac!" he said, having glanced around to check that no one was nearby.

"Ipecac?"

"In your coffee. It's the stuff all parents are supposed to have in their medicine cabinet. If your child eats some kind of poison, as long as it's a noncorrosive poison, you give them ipecac."

"So it's a nonpoison?"

"It's an emetic. Makes you barf."

"It does do that."

Now that McCoo had announced that the victim was presumed to be Gretzka, I could ask all the questions I wanted about him. It wouldn't seem strange for the new staff person to wonder who this guy was. But when I approached Nina, she remembered I had been asking earlier. She thought I had known even then that it was Gretzka who was killed, which is pretty true.

"You think Sophie Gretzka did it, don't you? That was why you were asking about her. How did you guess so early?"

Sophie as killer would fit with the face powder the trace evidence people found. And she was still missing. Say you and your husband plan to go to Florida for a vacation. He turns up dead. You vanish. You sure look like either the killer or a second victim.

But if she was dead, too, where was the body? And if she was alive, where had she gone?

I asked Nina again what Gretzka was like.

"He was precise. That's not a criticism; he ought to be precise. We're going to get catering recommendations, or not, on the basis of how well we do with each customer."

"You were more critical of him before."

"You think I'm doing one of those 'speak no ill of the dead' things? I'm not. I really liked him."

"Was he just a tough taskmaster all the time like you implied, though?"

"No. I'm trying to tell you. He had fun. He

181

joked. And he was kind. We had a new recruit named Peter once who dropped things. Now, you can't let that happen. We all thought the kid would be fired. I mean, one time we were carrying things to the van and poor Peter dropped a five-layer Bavarian cream cake with strawberries. The two guys following him slipped in the cream and dropped an orange-glazed chicken and twenty-four dessert plates."

"No! You're kidding."

"I am not. We all looked around at Serge. He closed his eyes and simmered for about sixty seconds. Then he told us to get more plates and some barbecued chicken from the deli and glaze it with orange marmalade to fill in for the chicken, and he went to tell Nick Lane to put together a five-layer cake out of sponge cake, to soak it in rum quickly, fill it with whipped cream and top it with strawberries. And *then* he said, '*Peter!*' Peter just cringed. He said, 'Tomorrow you will spend the whole day walking around with a book on your head and a water glass on each hand. And on the water glass will be balanced a cup."

"So Peter did this?"

"All the first day and after that for an hour in the morning and an hour before leaving work. After four days Gretzka put a plate on top of the cup on the water glass. After a week he put a cup on the plate on the cup on the water glass. Peter became brilliant. I mean, he got graceful and *deft*."

"Huh. Tell me more."

"Hey, I can't right now, Cat. Paul-Michel

said I could leave early. Nothing going on, so why not? And Jeff's picking me up."

"Jeff? What happened to Gregory? Or was it Cassius?"

"That was then. This is now."

I sat at my desk with a cup of coffee. A cup of coffee I would finish completely, not walk away from and leave half full and unguarded and come back to and carelessly drink.

Ipecac, huh? Unpleasant but not fatal. Not even possibly fatal, no matter how much you drink, since you can't keep it down.

Somebody was trying to scare me off, not kill me. Probably that's reassuring. Probably.

Three phone calls came in canceling parties, just in the first forty-five minutes I sat there. It was terribly depressing. The dollar bills had wings on them and were flying out Spenser and Angelotti's front door.

One caller said, "This is Mrs. Roving. You're doing a wedding brunch for me in three weeks. I'm thinking of canceling."

"Well, Mrs. Roving, I can assure you this horrible accident was no fault of Spenser and Angelotti. Someone broke in and killed a person here. It'll never happen again."

"Well, I'm not interested in that."

"You're not?"

"No. I want to know if you'll cater my brunch for half price."

Sighing, I said, "I'll have Mr. Angelotti call you back."

I had one call that morning that actually asked to schedule an affair.

"We're putting on a dinner for all our business associates," the man said.

"Excellent. Who is this?"

"My name is Bart Hohmeyer."

"So how many are you inviting, Mr. Hohmeyer?"

"I think a hundred and fifty."

"At a home or place of business?"

"At home."

"And you say you want dinner? For that many in a home, you would likely want a buffet. Or are you planning to rent tables and chairs?"

"Maybe. About the menu—"

"Yes? Well, you see, Mr. Hohmeyer, it makes a difference to the menu whether it's a sit-down dinner. It influences what your guests can easily handle. You don't want steak, or lobster in shells, for instance, if they're holding plates in their laps."

"Sit-down dinner. Because we want something special."

"Yes, Mr. Hohmeyer?" Was I hearing people muttering to him in the background?

"Yes. Special. This is the Chicago Coalition of Cannibals. We'd like a very special menu, and I'll tell you all about it. A standing rib roast, baby back ribs—"

There was uproarious laughter in the background.

"Strain the vegetables and the casserole juices through a fine strainer into a saucepan, pressing the juice out of the vegetables."

Now, this really and truly pissed me off. I snarled and spat epithets for about five minutes after Hohmeyer hung up amid gales of laughter. Finally, I realized that grumbling wasn't getting me or Bruno anywhere. I started to call friends.

"Hi, Jim," I said to James L. Spivvy, a paramedic and a buddy of mine. "You have years of experience with the terminally bloodied and moribund and better scientific sense than to worry that a dead body was found in a meat department, right?"

"Spenser and Angelotti?"

"Yes. They're nice people and they need help. Can you buy your groceries here today?"

"Sure."

With some other friends I used the ever effective "do it for me." With some I appealed to their sense of justice, saying, "Spenser and Angelotti are being punished for something they didn't do." I hoped this was true. I believed it was.

With some I said, "You owe me."

With a great many I said, "Through no fault of their own, they've had to reduce prices on perishables fifty percent. You'll never get as good a deal anywhere again. *Come and stock up.*"

With my aunt Ruth all I had to say was "Very major markdowns. Very."

And with all of them I rang off after laying the groundwork for a telephone-tree effect. "Tell your friends and tell them to tell all their friends."

I made several other calls, then asked Paul-Michel if I could leave for the day. He said, "What difference does it make?"

There was a lot of that feeling going around.

"As I said on the phone, Mrs. Cantabella, we're very concerned that our service be the best."

"It always has been," she said. She had taken me out onto her beautiful balcony overlooking Lake Shore Drive, and seated me with a glass of iced tea. She was wearing a black Armani suit, and now went on to explain that several of the wives of her husband's fellow executives were meeting her in an hour at the Art Institute. They were thinking of planning a benefit. She'd like us to cater.

I said, "Right now, with our—uh—unfortunate problem getting so much coverage in the media—"

"Ms. Marsala, I've been doing informal public relations for my husband's firm for twenty-five years. The memory of the public is very short. *Very* short. Does anybody refuse

186

to buy Tylenol? Seven or eight people were *killed* by sabotaged Tylenol. Do people eat Jack in the Box hamburgers after the *E. coli* disaster? Do they fly on TWA after Flight 800? You bet they do."

"You're right." The breeze from the lake picked up my hair and moved it around. In my apartment I could open the window and get the draft from the el when it swept past. I didn't envy her, though. She seemed to be always on display, groomed to perfection, twenty-four-hour advertising for her husband. I'd hate that.

Traffic hummed by on Lake Shore Drive, but it was far enough below so that it was a pleasant, distant sound of life. I could see Indiana from here and cotton clouds over the southern coast of Michigan far to the east.

Mrs. Cantabella said, "Please tell Bruno, who is a dear, by the way, that all he needs to do is hold on."

"You know we've lost Serge Gretzka, an important element in the business." Talk to me, Mrs. Cantabella.

"Serge was a very fine caterer. Very responsible. He wanted everything to be right. And everything always *was* right. Tell Bruno I said that. You never saw a bruised lettuce leaf or a dried-out shrimp in the curry when you had Spenser and Angelotti catering your dinner. Never so much as a dirty plate. But I think Gretzka is—was—the detail man, and Bruno has the palate."

"Well, I appreciate that—"

Just then Mr. Karl Cantabella came stamping

out of the back regions of the apartment, carrying a pigskin overnight bag and a black suede three-quarter-length coat over his arm.

"Polly! I can't find any ties with red in them."

"I sent three to the cleaner."

"Well, I need them *now*. I'm taking the shirts with the fine red line."

"The cleaner should have left them in the entry closet."

"Then go see if they're there, dammit." Polly jumped up to go look, leaving me and Mr. C. He stared balefully at me. "Who are you?"

"I'm from Spenser and Angelotti, Mr. Cantabella. We like to ask our clients whether our service has been to their liking."

"You mean you've got problems." He came closer. He was a big man, and he loomed over me. His heavy shoulders, the open neck of his shirt, which revealed wiry hairs on his chest, his scratchy but deep voice—he made me nervous.

"The problems weren't our fault and they're over, Mr. Cantabella."

He leaned toward me, so close I could smell his aftershave. "It's *not* over," he growled in my ear. I backed up to the balcony rail. "I couldn't hire you now," he said. "Think about it. Suppose I hired you. What am I going to tell my guests? We *think* this food is all right?"

I said, "Um," and slipped sideways, getting away from the railing.

He said, "You don't give a party in order to make your guests nervous. I'm into results. One mistake and you're out."

188

✧ ✧ ✧

"We meet once a month," Mark Zubro said. He was president of the Chicago Mystery Writers Association, the group Gretzka had catered on Friday night. "We have an after-dinner speaker. Always somebody who can give us ideas to use in future books or answer questions that mystery writers might have in a book they're working on, like ballistics or forensics. We've had a polygraph expert and a fingerprint expert so far this year." Zubro was in his early forties, a sympathetic-looking man with a Santa Claus beard.

"What was Friday night?"

"A poison expert."

"Yummy. And you have Spenser and Angelotti cater. Why not go to a restaurant?"

"We do sometimes. But quite often we go to lecture halls in local colleges and universities and invite students to come too, if they want."

"Why hire Spenser and Angelotti?"

"Two reasons. The food is better and the price is lower."

"Lower? I'm surprised." Whoops, not the right thing to say, as their employee. "I mean, I'm delighted to hear that."

"We had chicken with vegetables and dessert," Zubro said. "I don't cook, person-ally, so I don't know exactly what it was, but I know how to eat, and it was great. But it was chicken breast, and that just isn't all that expensive."

He was right. It was just chicken breasts,

not Kobe beef or Maine lobster, but it wasn't *just* chicken breast. I'd seen the menu. Chicken breast stuffed with prosciutto and fontina cheese and a whiff of lemon. For the vegetable, stir-fried fennel, mushroom caps stuffed with onion, celery, ham, and mozzarella. And rice. And for dessert, crêpes flamed in orange liqueur. Inexpensive ingredients prepared perfectly.

"So you were satisfied with our service?"

"Did you think we weren't?"

"No, we just conduct these service checks from time to time. I had heard there was some problem, but since I wasn't there—"

"The argument? Nothing about the food. It was about books before food dot com."

That's what it sounded like he said. I asked, "What?"

He spelled it out. "booksb4food.com is a Website where you can read about books. It describes the books and reprints a book review from a major publication. But a reader can also post his reaction to a book, whether he liked it or not."

"Is that important?"

As I hoped, he told me what had happened. I could see it all as he described it. Well, of course, he was a writer.

The group called Chicago Mystery Writers consists of writers, of course, as well as editors, reviewers, aspiring writers, and readers. They are all mystery enthusiasts.

During cocktails, which began at six-thirty, amid a lot of talk about some upcoming national awards, Henrietta Welles, who was the best selling writer in the group by a long chalk, had accused Fred Church of sabotage. About thirty people were standing around, when Henrietta, a short, pink, stout woman, said to Church, "You got on booksb4food and told them my book was terrible."

"I did not."

"Yes, you did. I had the address traced. It's yours."

Church was silent for a minute. The other people watched with a range of emotions, from horror to poorly veiled delight. Then Church said, "The book was past any suspension of disbelief. A gray market in body parts? I ask you! The fact is, you don't deserve your reputation."

"You're jealous!"

"And you, my dear, are a tubby, illiterate dwarf. In that book, you spell 'fluorescent lights' 'f-l-o-u-r-e-s-c-e-n-t' four times. You'd only have *flour*escent lights if you were setting your murder in a bakery."

She huffed. "Copy editors make mistakes."

"And the copy editor wrote miniscule with an 'i' for minuscule? As if it were a miniskirt?"

"You're being pedantic."

"And chaise lounge for chaise longue?"

Henrietta had started to say "What's wrong with chaise lounge?" but stopped herself in time.

"And you can riffle through papers, but not rifle through them. And it's sherbet, not sherbert."

"The copy editor—"

"Is a convenient whipping boy," Church continued, "And I suppose the copy editor made you put a silencer on a revolver? You are an undereducated, arrogant fake! You don't even have enough respect for your readers to bother with basic research."

At this point Henrietta may have stepped on Church's instep with her needle-sharp high heel. He shrieked. The other writers and guests quickly pulled them to opposite ends of the room. The two were then seated with friends at different tables and dinner proceeded. As the main course ended, the speaker started to talk.

"We have a lot of people who have to catch commuter trains, so we don't push for a late evening. We deprive the speaker of dessert," Zubro said, "although we let him or her eat it afterward, if they want."

"I heard there was an accident on the stairs."

Zubro looked at me sharply. "Certainly wasn't because of the food," he said astutely.

I smiled at his remark, but persisted. "I know. Just curious."

Zubro was far less amused about the argument than Nina had been. Unlike her, he did not think it was a hoot. He thought it was sad. He was a kindly person, and now he got serious indeed.

"Bault Hall is actually a Northwestern University School of Law moot-court room. We had several students come to the lecture. Which is good, but the place isn't set up well for dinners. The caterers brought their heavy stuff in by a small, slow freight elevator. When they left they carried the lighter things down the front steps. It's a long flight of stone steps."

"What happened?"

"Your Mr. Gretzka had discovered that Henrietta Welles was a pen name. Her real name is Emmy Ostojic. Their ancestors apparently came from the same place in eastern Europe. Moravia or Macedonia. I don't know where. I was busy trying to make sure the meeting was running right and all. And I was carrying a stack of dessert plates for the chef, Nina something. Anyhow, Gretzka and Henrietta walked down the stairs chatting together when they left."

"But with a lot of other people?"

"Oh, yes. Must have been thirty or so of us leaving all at the same time."

"What happened?"

"Henrietta just suddenly pitched forward down the stone stairs. As near as I could see, Gretzka was slightly in front of her, turning and talking to her when she fell."

"How close was—um—"

"Fred Church? Fairly close behind."

"Uh-uh. Was she badly hurt?"

"A compound fracture of the arm. You know, the kind of thing where the bone actually protrudes through the skin. It was pretty terrible. A lot of blood. And she has a concussion and a slight skull fracture. I've called the hospital twice a day. She's still in 'guarded' condition. I'm sure this tells you that we really enjoyed the food."

I ignored that. "And nobody saw Church—"

"Trip her? No. Nobody appears to have been looking at her right then."

Nobody but Gretzka.

"Delighted to see you my dear," Jerry Underhill said. Somehow I didn't like the idea of an undertaker being glad to see me. Immediately, I wondered whether I looked pale. Was there a telltale tremor in my fingers? Were the whites of my eyes turning yellow?

Jerry shook my hand, and then Jimmie shook my hand. They resembled each other quite closely, tallish, slender-bodied, dolichocephalic heads topped with mouse-colored, limp hair around a bald dome. Jerry was more strongly built, unless the effects of Jimmie's accident and long hospitalization had been to attenuate him. Jimmie spoke more shyly. Otherwise, I was reminded of the old Chase and Sanborn coffee ad: "What Mr. Chase didn't know about coffee, Mr. Sanborn did."

What Mr. Jerry didn't know about corpses, Mr. Jimmie did?

"Well, as I said when I called, I'm really here because Spenser and Angelotti wants to know whether they're serving their clients well. But I have some personal interest in finding a funeral home. I hate to talk about this, because my uncle Stick is still living. But he's seriously ill." Uncle Stick was gravely ill with obsessive Chicago Cubs addiction mania.

"I'm sorry to hear that," Mr. Jerry said,

194

sounding absolutely sincere. "We do have preneed plans."

Golly, aren't we all "preneed"?

"What an interesting name—Stick," said Mr. Jimmie.

"We kids called him that because he played stickball with us. And his first name is Stickney."

"Ah." Jimmie said "ah" better than anybody I'd ever heard. I guess years of practice with the bereaved will do that to you.

"Many people want to plan their own funerals and choose their own casket and so on," Jerry said. "Would your uncle want to come in and look at ours?"

"Oh, heavens, no! He doesn't want to even think about it!" Not in baseball season for sure. Or probably any other time. Stick was the kind of guy who liked to take his vacation at the same time and place as spring training. Plus, the Cubs opener was next week.

"I must tell you that The Brothers Funeral Home doesn't do cremation. We are in an area here where our clientele is largely Catholics and fundamentalist Protestants."

Jimmie said, "They don't believe in cremation. Many fundamentalist Christians believe in literal resurrection of the body at the last trump."

"I see. Well, I don't think Uncle Stick wants to be cremated anyway."

Jerry said, "Well, possibly I could give you a brochure about our services—"

Jimmie said, "And you might like to take a look at some of our caskets—"

"And our chapel of remembrance—" Possibly he forgot that I was familiar with it, having served cocktails there a few days back.

"And our menu of lovely floral blankets and tributes. We have an understanding with several florists in the area who can provide these in a wide range of prices—"

"—in any configuration your loved one would wish—"

"And the service you would wish—"

"And," I said, interrupting this catalog of delights, and trying not to picture carnations in the form of a baseball bat, "you must tell me if Spenser and Angelotti's service was what you had wished." Two could play at this game.

Thirty minutes later I had paged through a huge three-ring binder of floral tributes. I had scanned a folder of funeral layouts in four-color process on glossy paper. And now I was looking at an entire room full of caskets, a room larger than my whole apartment. All the coffins had the upper part open and the lower part closed, like they would be when the body was being displayed, as they usually were, from mid-chest up. Thus, you could see all the plush, cushioned, comfy fabric linings.

Jerry said, "Bronze is very tasteful for a man, don't you think?"

"Yes. What is this?"

Jimmie said, "Steel. Naturally the steel caskets are anodized in various finishes, to take away that steel look."

Jerry said, "But they are the very best for—"

"—permanence," Jimmie said. "Durability. We have twelve-gauge steel, sixteen-gauge—"

"And twenty-gauge."

"Is twenty-gauge the thickest?"

"No, twelve is the thickest. Now, this is a very fine casket."

"Oh, but isn't the wood on that one beautiful!"

"Not *on* it. It's *solid* cherry," Jerry said. "And this one is—"

"—mahogany," Jimmie said. "Now, this is oak, which is also very tasteful for—"

"—a man. But cherry is very masculine, too, in its own way. This particular lining, of course—"

"—you won't want. With the flowers. But it comes with plain white silk or ivory silk—"

"You won't want pink, of course."

I said, "Uncle Stick certainly would *not* want a pink lining. Or flowers. What is this?" There was a little knob set into the edge of the lid where the lower part of the coffin ended. I pulled it out. A little drawer.

"Oh, the remembrance drawer."

"For family photos—"

"—or a rosary—"

"—a lock of hair—"

I said, "It's not deep enough for a baseball."

"What?"

"Never mind." I took note of the prices, which ranged from thousands to many thousands. "I will tell the family about these. I personally think Stick would like oak."

They beamed. I said, "Now you promised to tell me how our service was."

"Oh, splendid," Jerry said. "I'm sorry the Spenser and Angelotti company is having such troubles."

"And did Serge Gretzka follow your instructions for the event?"

"I can't tell you that exactly," Jimmie said. "I wasn't back to work when Jerry planned it. But I can tell you the food was superb."

"And I can say it was exactly what I hoped," Jerry said. "Mr. Gretzka came to look at the facilities, and of course realized that we didn't really have kitchen facilities here. So he planned everything around that limitation."

"If Spenser and Angelotti could make my breakfast, lunch, and dinner," Jimmie said, "I would be a completely happy man."

"Me, too," said Jerry.

Last, I visited Sadler and Weiser. None of the partners could see me. A secretary with a red nose came in and told me she had been asked to "deal with" me.

"We are just checking to see that our service was all it might be," I said.

"Oh, I'm sure." She sniffled once.

"They enjoyed the food?" This was like pulling teeth.

"Probably."

"Um, well, you had a lot of new hires? Young people always have a good appetite."

"I guess."

"They're excited about being hired by such a big firm, though."

"Dupes."

"What?"

"The firm knows which ones they'll keep. They hire forty, work them eighty-five hours a week, ruining any hope of home life they might have, and then let thirty of them go."

"And they know which ones they'll keep right from the first?"

"The ones with connections."

"Do the recruits know?"

"Of course not."

"There's an actual list?"

"Yup."

I noticed she had brought two cloth bags out of her bottom desk drawer. I said, "Are you all right?"

"No," she sniffled. She pulled the top drawer out of the desk and poured everything in it into the bigger bag. I helped her hold it open.

"Are you leaving?" I asked.

"Been fired," she said.

I called McCoo before I left the office. There were a few things I'd have liked to know: For instance, did we have a cause of death yet? But his secretary told me he was out of town.

"So suddenly? He didn't tell me he was leaving."

There was brief silence, as if she wondered why I would ever imagine that McCoo had to keep me informed. But then she admitted, "It was sudden. His grandfather died, and he went to Omaha for the wake and funeral."

✧ 20 ✧

"Reduce the braising liquid to half its volume by boiling over high heat."

"I'm on one and a half split shifts today," Sam said, as we waited for Hermione to seat us for dinner.

"What in the world does that mean?"

"I'm on eight hours, then I get two hours off and I have to go back for four hours. I'm filling in for half of Tacoma's shift."

"She's on vacation?"

"She's sick, sort of. She was coming at a violent patient last night with a syringe of sedative. The patient hit her with the instrument tray and she fell and jabbed the sedative into her thigh and blitzed herself into tomorrow."

"That's terrible. Is she in bad shape?"

"No, just sleeping it off."

All of which meant we could eat dinner and then he had to be back at work. Same old same old.

We were waiting for a booth at Hermione's Heaven, the best restaurant in Chicago, called Hermione's for short of course. Hermione was a queen-sized woman who now approached the table at a queenly pace.

She wore a long dark skirt, a white silk shirt, and some glittery necklace of tiny mirrors that caught light and reflected it in sparkles around the room. "Major outfit!" I said.

"I call this my *Titanic* look," she said. "Black up to the deck, white above, and lots of lights. I'm a great ship on the seas of life."

"You are indeed." Hermione took no guff about her weight. Her view was that she was an adult and was entitled to run her own life. If she wanted to eat, she'd eat. She led us to a quiet booth in back. "What's good tonight?" I asked.

"All."

"Well, I mean especially good."

"All. However, the New Orleans–style salmon is tonight's special. Andouille sausage cooked with green, red, and yellow peppers, garlic, and onions, and tossed with risotto. Then topped with sweet-and-sour barbecued salmon."

Sam said, "Oh, well, when you make up something that sounds good, let me know."

"Hermione," I said, "do you get people in here who listen to some special or other and go, 'Yuk!'?"

"Sure. They're morons, of course. But something like fifty percent of the people in this country never eat fish. And half of those have never eaten fish in their *entire lives.*"

"But I mean, real yuk, like if you served caterpillars."

"Fried caterpillars are eaten in Mexico."

"Yuk."

"I serve frog's legs. I serve snails."

"That's a point."

We ordered the salmon.

Sam and I had talked a lot about honesty. Unfortunately, honest as we all want to be, what we honestly say about ourselves, believing it, and what we would do in a crisis are not necessarily the same. I love Sam, I really do, but I still had to test him.

"Sam, you know when I was shot at two nights ago?"

"Of course."

"Well, that wasn't the only thing."

"Uh-huh."

"The night before that, when I went to get my car at Spenser and Angelotti, somebody had broken out the windshield."

"Uh-huh."

"And the morning after the garbage got shot, I had left a cup of coffee on my desk at the store. I went away for about half an hour, and then when I went back and drank it, it made me violently sick."

"Immediately?"

"Pretty much."

"It sounds like ipecac."

"It was. How clever of you! I passed on the samples of the coffee and a pastry to Tim Savage and he had them tested."

Sam gave the whole thing some thought. Finally, he said, "It sounds more like they want to scare you away." I nodded. "Who has access to that office?"

"Only store personnel. They go back and forth in the hall all the time, to the staff lounge and the staff rest room."

"People from the public areas can't get in?"

202

"They could get in, but they'd be noticed. People like the Fern Ffolke use the public bathroom in the outer part of the store."

"Uh-huh. You think the killer is afraid you know something?"

"Or might stumble on something."

"Who was in the store that day?"

"Everybody. It was a normal workday. Normal at least if you allow for the murder. The same for the windshield thing. Pretty much everybody was there, and they had the whole day to do it in."

"What about the shooting?"

"McCoo looked into that. Spenser was home alone. Bruno Angelotti says he was still in the store ordering Italian ham, but nobody watched him do it. Kurt Westman, the head second-shift butcher, was at a line-dancing place, where people saw him, but most of them think they saw him earlier than when I was shot at. The first-shift butcher, Dack, went to a prizefight. Nobody saw him, but he had the ticket stub. Of course, the fight would have ended by then, but I think whoever it was had to have come early and waited there hoping I would come out. Paul-Michel Cartier, the assistant caterer, was home with his wife. But wives can lie and people can hire shooters. Nina Timko, who seems perfectly honest, says she was at home with a boyfriend. Probably a onetime boyfriend who wouldn't lie for her. The baker, Nicholas Lane, was clearly home. He says he ordered Chinese food delivered and the restaurant confirms that he received it. The rest of the staff, like the cashiers, janitors, bookkeeper, secretaries, and so on, are the same. Some had alibis; some didn't."

"Assuming somebody wants to scare you away, what *do* you know about the killer?"

"Not enough. I've been asking myself questions. Most of them are pretty desperate."

"Such as?"

"Well. Does the fact that the bones were packaged imply a particularly tidy personality? Somebody who likes to package everything?"

"Maybe. More likely it was a necessity."

"I agree. I'm pretty sure the killing happened this way: The killer met Gretzka at the store. Maybe he came prepared to kill. Maybe he wore gloves. We know now that there were no fingerprints in the butcher shop of anybody who didn't belong there. No fingerprints of cashiers, for instance, or the bookkeeper, or Spenser or Angelotti themselves. The detectives took fingerprints they believe to be Sophie Gretzka's from the kitchen at her home. There are none of hers in the butcher shop, either. And there were no mysterious fingerprints. Does that mean the killer wasn't an outsider? There wouldn't be fingerprints anyhow if the killer wore gloves. So either he planned to kill and wore gloves, or he lost his temper and grabbed up a knife and killed Gretzka and wiped everything clean when he was done. Lord knows that place is full of tools you can kill with. Or he's one of the staff. Anyway, the killer finds himself with a dead body. What does he do?"

Sam said, "He knows he doesn't have a whole lot of time."

"Right. He had from midnight at the very earliest to five A.M."

"You said the butchers didn't come in until seven."

"Sure," I said, "but would you want to be disposing of a dead body while half a dozen bakers were working in a room near you?"

"No. So, say he had five hours."

"Right. More likely four. There he—or she—is with a dead body. He probably has a car, but he's scared to take the body out of the store. Scared to drive around with it. And if he does take it out, maybe he can't think of anyplace to dump it."

Sam said, "Yeah. Getting rid of a dead body isn't easy."

"McCoo says it's the thing that trips up most killers most of the time."

"Even if you leave it in the trunk of a car at O'Hare, that's not going to help if it's your car."

"And worse if you get into an accident on the way. Okay. He thinks, wait a minute! They dispose of flesh and bones all the time here."

"There were drums that already had animal scraps in them."

"Yes. But if anybody looks in them, they can't be seen to have anything human inside. And people *will* look at them when they dump them into hoppers at the rendering yard. Somebody might notice."

"So he gets rid—" Sam suddenly got to his feet. "Come with me."

"What?"

He was pulling me by the hand toward the front door. As he walked, he called to Hermione. "Back in ten minutes!" She looked surprised but nodded.

"What are we doing?" I asked out on the sidewalk.

"We're going to talk about this while we walk around in the fresh air. And then we're going to go back inside and eat dinner *without* discussing this."

"Oh. I see."

"You were saying he disposes of the organs."

"Yes. Flushes them down the toilet in pieces, I think. Or down the garbage disposal. Small slices that go down easily. And puts flesh and small bones through the grinder so that they look like waste, spoiled stuff. And that goes into the drums. Bone pieces in the bone barrel. But not skin. Somebody might notice skin. That goes down the disposal."

"Not hair, though. It would clog."

"Or teeth," I said. "They might get caught in the trap, and if somebody came to clean it out, they'd be found."

"Right. He probably took the hair and the teeth away with him. Wrapped in butcher paper, maybe. Even if he was in an automobile accident, the package would be too small to be noticed. He could easily dispose of them later."

I said, "So why package the bones?"

"Too big to grind. Too big to carry home. And they looked, to him at least, just the same as beef bones. But how many people would know how to package the bones?"

"Sam, the automated packager is *such* a no-brainer. It says MORTON AUTOMATED PACKAGER in huge blue letters. There's an on-off button, with a red light next to OFF and a green light next to ON. You push ON and a screen comes up with a menu and instructions to 'click on product.' The product list is alphabetized. Go down to beef bones, click, and the belt carries your little white tray of bones into the machine and does the rest. Weighs, labels, everything."

"I see what you mean."

"Only somebody who had never *touched* a computer could possibly be stumped."

We began to walk around the block. I said, "So, after he finishes, he cleans up. Puts the bones in the meat case—no, wait, the alarm had been set. He couldn't have entered the hall without setting it off. All he could do without setting off the alarm is go out the back door."

Sam said, "So he puts the packaged bones on the shelves in the walk-in refrigerator. The morning staff would think the evening staff had packaged them. Somebody just moved them to the meat case in the morning."

"Of course. Gretzka would have had the key to the cold storage refrigerators. Then the killer cleans up the floor. And he washes the equipment. And he leaves."

"Exactly. And he leaves."

"And as far as he knows, no one will ever guess."

We walked all the way around the block, then came back to where we had started.

"Who would know how to cut up a body?" I asked.

"Who doesn't these days? Almost anybody who's been through an eighth-grade bio class."

"Anybody who watches the Discovery Channel."

"Anybody who watches *ER.*"

"Pretty much anybody."

"Plus, they weren't doing surgery. They didn't need actual anatomical knowledge."

The moment we returned to our booth, Hermione arrived with appetizers. Puff pastry filled with snails. Some people would think this particular delicious morsel was disgusting.

"Sam, we have to talk."

"What have we just been doing? When you say it that way, it sounds like bad news."

"No. It's just no news. About your proposal—"

"No news is bad news. Cat, will you marry me?"

"Listen, I do love you, Sam. But I'm not a young person anymore. I'm mid-thirties—"

"If you're saying I should find a younger woman, forget it. I don't want to try to talk over breakfast with someone who doesn't know who Jack Kennedy was. I'm not interested in teenagers."

Neither was I. Sam had laugh lines around his eyes, and some on his forehead that I thought of as life-experience lines. I liked to kiss them. I said, "No, that's not what I was going to say. The problem is that I'm kind of set in my ways. I'm used to living alone."

"When I come over to your place, we get along fine."

"Sam, let me finish. Besides living alone, I have been used to running my own life. One of the problems with John—and, mind you, it was only one of many—was that he wanted me to stop working."

"I would *never* ask you to do that!"

"No, but, see, he wanted me to stop working so that I wouldn't be out at night investigating things that sometimes people didn't want investigated. In other words, he didn't want me to take chances."

"Cat, you're a grown-up. You can run your own life."

"Sooner or later you'll try to tell me what to do."

"Do you think marriage consists of being told what to do?"

"Hey, what do I have to go by? My parents. My brothers and sisters-in-law. My friends. Sooner or later, you'll say, 'Don't do this story. It's dangerous. I'm stopping you for your own good.'"

"I *won't*. You don't tell me not to try to save an accident victim just because he has a communicable disease."

"No. But—I think you would stop me."

"That's not fair."

"No, it isn't, is it? But it's what scares me."

"You're an adult. You're allowed to make your own decisions. That's a matter of respect adults should give each other."

"Right," I said doubtfully.

I'm not totally stupid; I was very well aware that Sam is much more of a "catch" than I am. He's a surgeon. I'm a hand-to-mouth under-paid writer whom my uncle George would describe as "past her first youth." But then, Uncle George is the sort of person who will say a woman is "twenty-six but still attractive."

The thing is, when you get close to marriage, relationships change. It had happened to John and me; he had wanted me to stop working. He was an intelligent, sensitive, helpful, kind, good man who wanted me to *quit.* As you become more and more inter-dependent, the man gets protective. And it's natural. It's even admirable, probably. Maybe women do, too. Would I want someone I loved to be in danger?

But I actually *like* my life. So shoot me!

"How can I prove to you that I'm not John?"

How indeed?

Sam had done pretty well when I told him about the windshield and the ipecac. And he'd not said a word about how I should avoid getting shot at in the future. Not a word about how I should look for a job in book-binding or lawn maintenance. We'd see how he did on the really big test.

"Remove the bones from the oven. Pour the reduced sauce over the shanks, for a shiny glaze."

After I left Sam I made a call.

"Tim? Meet me out back of the store in forty-five minutes."

The detective said, "Hey, I've been thinking. I could get in trouble for this."

"You knew that when you agreed."

One thing I had realized today. Bruno and Paul-Michel had told me when I first took the job at the store that caterers heard a lot of things from customers that the caterers didn't talk about. Bruno said, "A caterer is like a priest."

I knew cops had an unblinking, frank, and oddly intimate view of the city. So did paramedics. They went everywhere and saw and heard things that normal citizens never do. So do medical examiners.

But caterers? I had never realized they saw and heard a lot more than they could tell.

It was now 8 P.M. Nina's home number was in the catering contact file. I called her.

"Um, huh?" she said into the phone. Then

211

she giggled. In the background I heard a man's voice mumble.

I didn't ask her what she'd been doing. "Nina? This is Cat Marsala from the store."

"Oh, uh, hi."

"Hi. Just one quick question. Did Gretzka talk much about things he heard at the last few places he went to cater?"

"Well, sure, Cat. You hear all kinds of stuff."

"Tell me anything you remember him saying about the Cantabellas, the Underhills, the mystery writers, or the Sadler and Weiser people."

"Jeez! There was so much. Let's see. He said he didn't see Jimmie Underhill, because he was still in rehab, and Gretzka hoped Jerry's choice of dinner would please him. I told you about the writers. Nothing much at the lawyers except they were snotty. Somebody was passing around a list of some sort and they were snickering. And Cantabella—uh, that guy really upset him."

"Why?"

"He overheard Cantabella talking to his lawyer. Mr. C.'s gonna divorce Mrs. C., he said, but they were worried about what she'd get. Money, I mean. There was this corporate wife in the news recently who got half her husband's money. I mean, like, she argued that she'd spent yea number of years entertaining for him, dinners for his friends and bosses and so on. Like an unpaid social secretary, doing nothing but, full-time. See what I mean?"

"Perfectly."

"And then he dumps her, so it took twenty

years of her life, now she wants to be paid, she earned it, and the judge said okay. So Mr. C. wants to avoid this with Mrs. C. And so he doesn't want her to know that he's going to dump her until he 'gets his ducks in a row.' That was what he said, ducks in a row. Which I guess means that he wants to accuse her of something or frame her for something or hide his assets more likely, and he'll never get away with it if she knows this is coming down the pike. You understand?"

"Oh, yes. I understand very well. Why did he want to dump her, do you know?"

"Yeah. Too old."

"Hell. A lot of men are like that. Couldn't he just have an affair?"

"Not *this* guy. He said it was for business reasons. Clients like to see a young, pretty hostess. Mrs. C. was past it, he said, and Gretzka was all, like, 'What should I do about this?' because he thought Mrs. C. was a real lady, and he admired her, if you see what I mean."

How frustrating. I thought I knew who the killer was. But I was only 90 percent sure, not a hundred. And I couldn't imagine any way to prove it. Any safe, legal way.

Tim said, "Remind me why I'm doing this."

"Because you're a risk-taker."

"No, I mean why here? Why now?"

"I just can't narrow it down any more."

I said, "This whole situation reminds me of a song my grandfather sings."

Tim Savage and I were in my car heading north from the Spenser and Angelotti parking lot. Tim was wearing a black jacket, black pants, black running shoes with black socks, and had a black knit stocking cap in his hand. He said, "Raiding a suspect reminds you of a song?"

"No, the butcher shop reminds me of it. I think it was some 1890s humorous ditty, or something."

"Go ahead. Tell me. You will anyway."

"Nice of you to ask. It goes like this."

I sang:

Oh, Mr. Dunderabeck,
How could you be so mean?
For cats and dogs,
And mice and hogs
Will never more be seen.
They've all been ground to sausage
    meat
In Dunderabeck's machine.

"Not bad. You can't sing, of course, but that's not your fault. Some got it, some don't got it. The song reminds me of my aunt."

"She made sausage?"

"No. She had a saying. 'Sausage is delicious, but you don't want to see it being made.' What she meant, besides the literal fact that things go into sausage that you don't want to know about, is that you don't always need to know what's behind everything."

"She couldn't have been a cop."

"Or a reporter."

"Damn right."

I pulled the Bronco to a stop half a block down from our target. "Let's test the equipment," I said.

"It's good stuff. I've had it three years."

"Let's test it anyway."

"You're a hard woman."

"Damn right again. Tim, you know those movies where, after a series of killings, the heroine gets an idea and goes out into the deserted graveyard in the night? Nobody to back her up? Tells nobody she's going? Then she's attacked and she's completely amazed that there's danger? Well, that's dumb. It's lame for the movie and it's stupid for the heroine."

"Well, of course."

"So don't you do that. You're my backup. And if anything goes bad, you call for backup for *yourself* before you come in, okay?"

"Sure. I got my radio."

"Great. Then nothing can possibly go wrong."

"Ooooo! Never say that."

"I was joking."

The night had the wet, sweet coolness of spring. I walked a quarter block away, in the opposite direction from our quarry. Then I said, angling my mouth toward my chest, "Wave if you hear me, Tim."

A hand rose above the hedge and semaphored.

I walked back toward my goal. Two people came out the front door, but it was now nine-thirty and there shouldn't be any others. I strode briskly up the sidewalk and pushed open the door. I went in.

✦ 22 ✦

"Sprinkle the top with the *gremolata.*"

"Good evening, Mr. Underhill."

"Miss Marsala!" Jerry Underhill was wearing his dark blue suit, white shirt, and red-and-white-striped tie, the undertaker's uniform. His bland, professionally sympathetic face gave nothing away. "What can I do for you?"

"We need to talk."

He glanced into the viewing room to our left, where I could see Jimmie Underhill chatting with two relatives of the deceased. The relatives were putting on coats and shifting feet like they were getting ready to leave.

The secretary was just visible from the back in the casket room. She was already wearing her coat. As I glanced, the casket room lights went out. "Follow me," Jerry said, opening a hall door.

And I did. He had got me out of the reception area before the secretary or Jimmie had seen me. That was fine. It was exactly what I wanted. To put it another way, I wanted him to think our conversation was private.

The hall led to some back offices, including one with file cabinets and a metal desk puddled with papers. Jerry, however, made a quick turn and gestured to a stairway leading down.

"Let's talk in the basement," he said.

"Sure." I wanted him to feel safe.

The basement workroom was all stainless steel and tile, just like the medical examiner's office and just like the butcher shop. The principal difference here was that there were more floor drains. The walls were pale gray tile, presumably not white because white would reflect too much glare from the large panels of fluorescent lights set into the white acoustical ceiling. There were four stainless steel utility sinks, three stainless steel tables, with a body under a plastic sheet on one, cabinets of tools and supplies all along two walls, a white tile floor, and some autoclaves for sterilizing instruments. There was also an open steel-fronted appliance that looked like an industrial dishwasher.

"Jeez! I wish I owned some stock in stainless steel companies!"

"What?"

"Never mind."

The body lay on the center table. Jerry Underhill whipped the sheet off, saying, "You can talk to me if you want, but I have to work. We do about two to three funerals every day."

If he was trying to scare me, he'd picked the wrong person. The naked body under the sheet was that of a woman possibly seventy-five or eighty years old. "See, we work at night a lot," Jerry Underhill said. "If your elderly aunt Agnes dies in her retirement home this afternoon, you probably want the relatives to be able to come and 'view the remains' by tomorrow sometime, don't you?"

"I suppose I do."

Jerry turned on an exhaust fan. "We have to keep up to OSHA standards," he said, smiling, as he pulled on surgical gloves.

"Absolutely."

"This is a nice, clean body," he said, picking up an aerosol spray bottle. He sprayed a coating over the top surface of the woman, rubbing it with a cloth to distribute the fluid evenly. He turned the body over and did the same with the back.

"She's been living in an expensive retirement home. They do a nice job of washing the deceased." He left her turned on her stomach. "We want any fluid from the mouth to drain out. We call it 'purge.' "

I noticed some purplish discolorations of the back and shoulders. These were not bedsores or evidence of any injury. They were livor mortis, blood pooling in the low places.

While the mouth was draining, he moved the arms and legs, massaging them and bending them. "I can relieve the rigor mortis to quite an extent this way." After a few minutes, he turned the body right side up and wiped inside the mouth with swabs of stuff that gave off a smell of disinfectant. Then he packed the mouth with gauze. "Now, what did you want to talk about?"

"Serge Gretzka. He had a very hands-on approach to his job."

"Somewhat like me." Jerry laughed, patting the old woman's naked thigh.

"That's right. He always visited the places where the event he was to cater would take place. That way he would know what cooking or reheating facilities were available and how much supplementary equipment he would need and so on."

"Thorough. I admire that. We were very pleased with his work. I know exactly how it is to hope the customer will appreciate your artistry. This lady, for example. Her nose is just a touch off center."

He inserted a cotton plug in one side, jamming it in hard with a probe until the nose evened out. Then he selected a rechargeable razor from the tray and shaved hairs and down from her face.

Picking up two hemispheres of plastic, covered on the convex side with small bumps, he said, "See these? We call these 'eyecaps.' " Firmly he pulled back the woman's eyelids and forced the caps directly over the somewhat sunken eyeballs. When he dragged the eyelids down over them, the bumps held the lids in place. "If they don't stay, I'll Superglue them," he said.

Superglue is everywhere I go this week, I thought. Superglue and stainless steel.

"Eyes are very important. The upper and lower lids should meet two-thirds of the way down. If they're higher, the body looks like it's in pain.

"Now watch. This is where the artistry comes in." He took a curved metal plate about three inches long and one inch wide with sharp spikes on the outside and placed it inside her mouth over the teeth. When he pulled the lips down over it, the spikes inside held them in position.

"The mouth is terribly important," he said. "It mustn't close too tightly. If it's puckered it looks disapproving. If it's too loose, well, it looks like the person's dead. Can't have that." He pulled the lips around a bit, cocked his head, checked from several positions. Satisfied, he picked a threaded, curved needle from the tray and sewed the lips together.

"So when Gretzka visited these places, he often—"

"I can Superglue the lips too, if they don't hold. There will be tissue changes over the next two days of viewing. Despite the humectants in the embalming fluid, the body does begin to dry out. Now, let me show you how we access the arteries for embalming."

"Gretzka overheard something as he went about his work. Something that worried him."

"We hear a lot, too. You can't imagine the things the bereaved relatives sometimes blurt out. Old feuds. Scandals. Even crimes."

He rolled the tray over to the table. There were scalpels and long hollow steel tubes he called trocars on it. "There are four types of embalming. The most important are arterial embalming and cavity embalming, in which we inject preservatives into the abdominal cavity. The other two are hypodermic embalming, where we just inject chemicals into certain needy areas that didn't get reached by the arterial, and surface embalming, which is nothing more than applying chemicals to the skin as liquid or gel."

"How nice."

"The primary preservatives are formaldehyde and methyl alcohol. Embalming hardens the muscles. After eight to ten hours the muscle fibers are set, and we can't move the limbs much anymore, so we like to get the body into its viewing position soon after the process starts." He lined up the legs demurely, but moved both arms so that the hands hung down over the sides of the table.

"That's so the fluid reaches the hands," he said. "Clothes go on last. Don't want liquids on them. If the body is too stiff, we can always slit the clothes in back."

He picked up a scalpel and slashed quickly into the neck, in less than two minutes exposing both carotid arteries and both jugular veins. "We can do this differently in young women who want to wear a low-cut dress." He sliced through the esophagus and trachea. Then he tied the lower ends of both with gauze. "Don't want burps as gases form, now, do we?"

He attached clear tubing to both carotid arteries and attached the other ends of the tubes to a five-gallon jug, which was about three-quarters full of fluid. Two other tubes went into the jugular veins, but he left these loose.

"She's not a big lady. She'll take about three gallons, I think," he said, flicking a switch on a stainless steel mechanism underneath the jug.

"This is a centrifugal pump," he said. "It pushes the fluid into the arteries at a pressure of ten pounds per square inch."

"Why is the fluid pink?"

"That's dye to help put back the pink of life. There are some anticoagulants in it too, and perfume."

As the pump came up to pressure, the blood began to drain from the jugulars by gravity into drains in the floor. He placed a U-shaped block under the head, raising it slightly, and tilted it a bit toward the right. He cleaned the woman's fingernails quickly.

"Most bodies are viewed from the right, so you turn the face to the right. You raise the torso just a bit to make the deceased appear comfortable. The hands need to lie comfortably across the chest. The fingers need to look relaxed. If they tend to splay out I can always—"

"Superglue them?"

"Exactly! What a quick learner you are! These are bruises, see? Probably from leaning on bed rails," he said, pointing to discolored splotches on her left arm. "We usually can remove bruises with 'Bruise Bleach.'" He applied this with a gauze pad.

"What is it made of?"

"Carbolic acid. The easiest bodies to deal with are the ones who kill themselves with carbon monoxide. It gives them a rosy color, so we don't need much dye in the fluid. And, of course, there's no damage to the surface of the body that needs repair. They're the best!"

He stood back to see how the bruise bleaching process was working.

"Now this," he said, picking up a long hollow stainless steel tube, "is what we use for cavity embalming. We take a stronger solution of embalming fluid, insert this instrument into the abdominal cavity"—here he pushed it inside the woman with a hideous sound like puncturing a Mylar balloon—"and bathe the internal organs in preservative."

"When Gretzka was here, he overheard something."

"By early morning she'll be completely perfused," he said, forcing in the fluid. "And then we'll start the hairdressing and final cosmetic process."

"So I guess this isn't a body you can steal the corneas or skin grafts from."

Jerry froze for two seconds. Then, relaxing, he said, "What a terrible accusation. You've got me wrong."

"Gretzka asked about it. The day before he died, he asked one of the store owners what the regulations were on dead bodies."

"Oh, come on! The 'regulations' are such that I can't do things like that."

"Serge was a precise person. Moral. Everybody describes him as very concerned with what was right. He wouldn't have overlooked what you're doing."

"So you say. Maybe he asked about regulations because he intended to kill somebody, and when he tried it, maybe that person retaliated and killed him."

"I doubt—"

Suddenly he whipped around and clouted me in the face with the embalming pump. Fluid flew everywhere. As I staggered back, he pulled the trocar from the woman, brandished it, and shouted, "Maybe *this* will be the best thing to do to you. Inject you full of formaldehyde."

He jumped back and locked the lab door.

Okay, Tim. Time to call for backup.

I said, "You've been stealing corneas and selling them. And skin. Cadaver skin is used for covering burn patients. Serge Gretzka overheard your meeting with your buyer. Maybe he heard over your speaker system in the break room."

"You don't know any such thing." He was stalking me with the trocar.

"I looked up organ grafts. Organs like kidneys and hearts have to be used fresh from the donor. But not what they call 'tissue grafts.' Bone, skin, corneas. In fact, I read on the 'net that bone can be freeze-dried and used years later. A funeral home must be a gold mine. You have a black market in tissue."

"There is no black market."

"There's a gray market in human tissue. Half of the states in this country allow hospital pathologists and funeral directors to remove corneas *without the permission of the family*. Put an 'eyecap' in and no one will ever know. The way the money is made is simple. They charge big fees all the way along the line for 'service costs.' Same with bone. Who would know that Aunt Agnes, in her half casket, had broom handles instead of leg bones, just like an Egyptian mummy? Same for skin. It's taken from the back of the cadaver, and who will ever see that? It takes six to eight cadaver back skins to get a burn victim through the first few weeks. It would be a good deed, Jerry, if you didn't do it secretly, for the money."

Jerry Underhill looked like a man who was thinking hard. He must realize, as he had with Gretzka, that once the question was asked, tracing the illegal sale of body parts would not be difficult. He would be financially ruined and criminally prosecuted, even if he was not convicted of Gretzka's murder.

"You realize you've sealed your death warrant," he said.

Great, Tim! You've got it on tape. Now's the time to come breaking in.

Jerry said, "I don't do any sensitive stuff. That's the key. If somebody gets a heart-lung transplant, everybody gets all excited. They want to thank the donor's family and make an emotional big deal of it. But have you ever heard anybody getting excited about a skin graft?"

"You didn't bring Gretzka's body back here because you didn't want it in the car, that little sports car you drive. Naturally you

225

couldn't take the hearse to the store at night. That *really* might be noticed. You knew you couldn't get rid of a body easily. You knew there isn't enough space in a casket to put in another body. And you don't do cremations. But the biggest reason was, you were covered with blood. You put Gretzka's clothes on over yours, to get them out of the store, but they were even bloodier than yours. You didn't dare have a body in the car if you were stopped by police."

"And I wasn't."

He scared me. Jerry Underhill was a lot taller than I am—well, almost everybody is. He was not especially hefty, but he lifted and shifted dead bodies all day. Deadweight. He was stronger than he looked. If Tim didn't get in here fast, Jerry could kill me and all Tim would find was my body.

Tim, where the hell are you?

I said, "And for that reason, I wonder if you weren't *so* scared in the car that you didn't dare even to throw the teeth and hair out along the way. I'll just bet you were too scared to stop on a bridge and drop them into the water and chance being seen. My guess is, your instinct would be to get home here as fast as possible. You could easily have pushed them into a coffin. Or—I wonder if the police could maybe find them in the cemetery in one of the clients you buried Saturday, in one of those memory drawers!"

Jerry leaped at me and we fell back against the second table. He pounded at my head. Maybe I was still dizzy from the first blow from

226

the pump, because I fell down. He hit me again, while I lay there, confused, and a second later—it couldn't have been more—I realized he was running duct tape around my wrists, taping them together.

"Heh! Yeah!" he said happily. "You know the old Archimedes saying that if you have a lever long enough you can move the world?"

"That's not exactly what he said—"

"And I say, with enough duct tape you can bind up the planet!"

This guy was nuts. *And where the hell are you, Tim? This has gone on long enough. You don't have to wait for all the cavalry to arrive.*

"They found your powder at the murder scene you know."

"What?"

"The cosmetic powder you use on your corpses. Probably there was some on your clothing. I thought at first it meant Sophie Gretzka killed her husband. But it was an unusual type. It will eventually be identified as undertaker stuff."

I hope. Come on, Tim!

"We'll just have to take that chance, won't we? I'm not going to be any worse off than I am now." He attached a bag of fluid to a tube and the tube to a trocar. Then he came toward me.

Tim, this is no joke!

To make this perfectly clear to Tim at the other end of the radio beam, I yelled, "Help! Help!"

"Nobody will hear you. The room is sound-proofed."

"Your brother Jimmie might," I said. "I think Jimmie was on to you. He suspected. So you sabotaged his car, and he had the accident. But it didn't kill him, the way you hoped. Almost, but not quite. It must be very difficult to steal body parts with an innocent partner liable to walk in at any moment. It must restrict your opportunities."

There was a knock at the door. Then the knob rattled. Then I heard a key turn outside. "Thank God!" I said. "Help!"

The door opened and Jimmie Underhill stepped in, with that puzzled look he so often wore.

"Help!" I yelled.

Behind him staggered Tim Savage, blood running down his cheek near his ear, his hands bound to the sides of his body with a rope.

"Look what I found hiding in the bushes," Jimmie Underhill said.

✦ 23 ✦

"Serve with a special long, narrow spoon, designed to eat the marrow of the bones."

"I had to hit him with the shovel," Jimmie said.

"Well done," said Jerry.

"Not very couth, though."

"One does what one must, Jimmie."

"And I have his gun."

"Oh, very well done, Jimmie."

"If we only did cremation this would all have been so easy! That's your fault, Jerry. Though I don't mean to criticize."

"There wasn't much market for cremation, Jimmie. Our Catholics don't approve. And the equipment is terribly expensive."

"I know. Needs a lot of space, too."

"Makes the neighbors nervous. Think any smoke they smell is Uncle Jack."

"Health department constantly on your back," Jimmie said.

"This has become awfully complicated, Jimmie." Jerry turned to me and Tim. "I think we'd better put you both in storage until we decide exactly what to do with you."

I studied Tim's condition more closely. There was a lot of blood all down his neck and onto his shirt. The shovel had caught him on the head right over the top of his left ear. But it looked like the flat of the shovel had hit him, not the sharp edge. Otherwise he'd probably be dead.

Jerry pulled Tim's hands to the front and wrapped duct tape around them. Then he took off the rope. Throughout this process, Jimmie held Tim's gun trained on him.

"I'm sorry, Cat," Tim said.

"Come on. Move!"

Jerry pushed us into a cool storage locker just off the workroom. "We'll just close up shop," he said.

"Good thinking, Jerry," Jimmie said. "No weapons in here for them."

Jerry said, "Be right back."

Jimmie said, "Stored in the storeroom. Isn't that appropriate?"

"And you'll have a little company."

Jerry whipped a plasticized sheet off a body lying on a stainless steel gurney. It was a man about thirty-five years old. He had clearly been autopsied, since the torso was sewn back up with coarse black sutures and I could see some suture thread at the back of the head. The reason he'd been autopsied was obvious. He was a victim of violence. Lots of violence. He'd been dismembered. The head was attached to the torso, but the arms and legs had been hacked off. Also some parts we might not want to talk about.

Jerry waved his hand to introduce the man. "This here is Johnny Three-Fingers

Campeau. He got into a debt problem. Stole from the mob, and when they found out, he just went all to pieces."

I said to Jerry, "This isn't going to work. You'll have the same problem, how to dispose of a corpse. Except this time you'll have two."

"Not exactly the same problem," Jerry said.

"No need to transport the body," Jimmie said.

I said, "But you can't just bury a body without papers."

"A piece in each coffin, I think," Jerry said.

"Yes, one leg with Mrs. Burt, half a torso with Mr. Campeau."

"Take about fourteen funerals to get rid of you both."

"Less than a week," Jimmie said.

"Patience pays off," Jerry said.

I said, "But we'll be missing. The cops will come looking. And they'll be rabid, because a cop will be missing."

"No evidence. They won't be able to get a warrant."

"Plus, we won't be any worse off than we are now, will we?"

"You'd best make friends with Mr. Campeau. You'll be spending lots of time together."

Red with fury, I yelled, "Hey! You know what? You want to scare me with a dead body? You can't get to me that way. I am really not doing disgust anymore. I don't think blood is disgusting. Or guts! Or feces or barf. They may be sanitation problems, but they're not disgusting. I'm completely over that. What's disgusting to me is murder. And cruelty. And your utterly self-centered greed. Now *that's disgusting*!"

"Darling speech," Jerry said.

"Won't save you," Jimmie said.

"Cool off a little while."

"Get a start."

"Yes, you'll be room temperature soon."

I pulled Tim's tape off with my teeth. He pulled my tape off with his hands, which was probably less painful. A little.

"What good does this do?" he said. I knew he was embarrassed. "They have my gun."

"I'm not sure." I looked around the storeroom, but it was totally plain. White tile walls, no instruments, not even any pipes or wiring. "There's nothing here to use as a weapon."

There was a grate in the ceiling where the cold air was coming in. I said, "Boost me up."

Standing on Tim's cupped hands, I seized the grate and pulled. It bent in the middle and came off so fast I almost fell over backward. The thing wasn't much sturdier than aluminum foil.

"It's hopeless," Tim said.

"Well, there's a last time for everything."

We heard a sound in the outer room. Then a key in the door. Tim said, "They're going to kill us!"

"Wait. We do have a weapon."

The door flew open. I shoved the rigid torso at Tim, who was bigger than I and could hold a heavy battering ram. When Jerry fired at Tim, he used the torso as a shield. I grabbed a leg, with some rigor still in it, and when the shot *ka-chunked* into the torso, I cracked Jerry over the head with the leg as hard as I possibly could.

❖ 24 ❖

"Serve with risotto Milanese and a robust red wine."

"You've got it all wrong!"

The arresting officers cuffed Jimmie's hands behind his back with no trouble. But Jerry writhed and kicked and tried to break away.

"You can't do this! It was an accident. It was self-defense," he screamed. "Gretzka was going to blackmail me. I said no and he attacked me. He hit me! He—he—bludgeoned my face and body with a meat tenderizer mallet."

"So you cut him up?" I asked.

"Only to hide him. He fell and hit his head. I was afraid I'd be blamed."

"He hit you?"

"Yes, he hit me maybe a dozen times. Smashed my head into the wall."

"Gee, then you'd almost think there would've been human blood on the walls instead of just the floor."

"He almost broke my nose!"

"Hmmm. That was just four days ago. If he hit you, where are the bruises?"

"Uhhhh—"

"I bet he's using Bruise Bleach," I said.

When I woke up in the morning, feeling very much like Superperson, I immediately phoned Sam to say I'd meet him for lunch. Then I went to check on Long John Silver.

In his cage was an egg.

What? I thought I was hallucinating.

Long John? Oh, my!

"LJ, what's going on?" An *egg*?

LJ didn't say anything, only flew away to the curtain rod.

Was this egg our new baby? Was I going to be a stepmother? No. Wait. Of course not. No, I knew it couldn't be fertilized. He was the only parrot in the place. Or *she* was.

Long Jane Silver?

Already a little shaky from the parrot egg, I went out to meet with McCoo, just back from his family obligations in Omaha.

He said, "Jimmie is turning state's evidence."

"Oh! I thought he and Jerry were so close. Joined at the hip practically."

"Apparently being joined at the hip is sometimes constraining. Jimmie says he didn't kill anybody. True. Says Jerry's a hothead. True. He says Jerry went to Spenser and Angelotti to bribe Gretzka. Probably true."

"Everybody tells me Gretzka was very moral."

"Exactly. Jimmie says Gretzka turned him down. But Jimmie says—get this—Jerry took a pair of gloves with him."

"Premeditation."

"In a word, yes."

I said, "You know, they fit the psychological profile I had in mind. Who would believe they could get away with human bones in the meat case? Who of all people would be so aware that people simply *don't think of things* that bother them? Undertakers."

He said, "You're right. They see denial every day in their work."

"The very fact that people refuse to imagine distasteful things made the crime possible. Think of Jimmie and Jerry growing up. They'd be teased by their friends. They'd be called names by the other kids at school. Ghoul. Vampire. After all, they lived over their father's funeral home."

"You're not feeling sorry for them, I hope."

"Not exactly. Although society wants people to do these things for us, and at the same time we want to be able to despise them for it. What I'm saying is that Jimmie and Jerry would know, because of their whole life experience, how people avert their minds. They'd realize it more than doctors, more than anybody. A funeral director goes through life with *everybody he meets* trying not to think of what he does. And succeeding."

McCoo said, "They would assume that nobody would even imagine that bone in the meat case was human."

"And they were right. Nobody did."

"If it hadn't been for Sam."

"Darn right. Every experience all their lives would lead them to think that nobody understands, nobody sees, and, for sure, nobody cares. A lifetime of that and they'd think nobody faces up to anything."

Before I left to go to Spenser and Angelotti I said, "McCoo? Who leaked word about the bones in the meat case?"

He hesitated. "This is confidential."

"All right."

"Please don't pass this on. Albert Honneker is very sad about it. He trusted all his people. We did a little poking around and discovered that Chet Parker had run out and bought a car on Tuesday. A tomato red Porsche. When somebody starts spending a lot of money—"

"Chet? The cute young evidence tech?"

"He's admitted it. He contacted that guy Etheridge, who wanted a scoop so as to get an offer from New York. Etheridge is rumored to have money, and I guess it's true. He certainly gave Chet big money for the exclusive."

I went to the store. Their business was recovering slowly. I think my calls had helped. Bruno Angelotti, having overcome Spenser's continual objections to increasing the number of items, was now stocking several new brands of food for vegans, people who eat no meat, nor any meat products at all. The olive oil lady, who was actually the food instructor, had a group of ten on the chairs in front of her and was following this line of thought: "You can have complete protein in your diet, even if you are a vegetarian," she said. "All you need to do is consume both legumes—peas, beans, lentils, and so on— and grains, such as wheat, corn, rice, and millet. Legumes have certain amino acids that grains lack, and grains have the others that legumes lack. Together they make the building blocks of all protein. This is probably why so many traditional dishes around the world contain both. Beans and rice. Corn and peas. And so on. Today we will make three such recipes from around the world—*porotos granados,* red beans with corn and squash from Chile, steamed rice with dill and lima beans from Iran, and *risi e bisi,* rice and peas, from Italy."

I didn't hang around to hear more. I was heading for Bruno's office.

Spenser, I knew, was kicking up a fuss, demanding that the city reimburse him for the cost of recalling the meat products. His reason seemed to be that the city had failed in its promise to keep the reason secret. Ever the cost cutter.

Ducking into Spenser's office, I said, "Meet me in Bruno's office. Now." When they were both there, I closed the door.

"Sit down," I said coldly.

Spenser was huffy at my tone, but Bruno said, "Cat saved us, Henry. The least you can do is give her a few minutes."

I said, "I was attacked three times. One: my car windshield was broken. Two: I was shot at. Three: my coffee was poisoned. Then the attacks stopped. There was so much going on that I didn't notice it at first exactly when they stopped."

Bruno said, "Oh, my God! You never told me you were attacked."

Spenser said, "So? The killer was found."

"It wasn't the killer. The attacks stopped well before the killer was found. They stopped when the secret about the bones in the meat case leaked out to the press. They never happened after the media showed up here at the store."

"That means—um, what does that mean?" Bruno asked.

"The attacks had confused things because I thought the killer was after me. And only somebody familiar to store personnel could get to the catering office unnoticed to poison my coffee, and therefore it most likely would have to be one of the staff." I looked at Henry Spenser. "It was you."

"It was not!"

"You didn't want me here from the first. You kept telling me the police would find the killer, but at the same time you said you didn't really think they would. There was no evidence to speak of. They wouldn't be likely to solve it. But you were afraid that I might. Hanging around the store, I might work out relationships that led to murder. You thought the killer was Nicholas Lane, who you realized was in love with Sophie Gretzka. So you tried to scare me off."

"I wanted the killer found!"

"No, you didn't. If the killer was found, word would get out immediately that there had been human bones in the meat case. And later, if it was solved, everybody would be reminded all over again when the details came out at a big media trial."

He stared at me, anger building. Finally he exploded.

"Well, of course! How stupid could you be? Did you think I actually *wanted* you to find the killer? What the hell do I care who did it? It was done. Over! If I could've waved a magic wand and brought Gretzka back, it would only have been moral to do so. But I couldn't do that."

"Right."

"We could have the best food in the *world* at the best prices in the city, and nobody would come. And we would be bankrupt."

"Yes."

"I never wanted it solved! Wasn't this obvious to Bruno and you? Wasn't this obvious to everybody?"

I didn't want to hurt Bruno. I left it to them to work it out.

I did not tell McCoo.

Did I ever think that Nina was the killer? No. I didn't think there was time in her busy social life.

And it couldn't be the Fern Ffolke, because they would have leaked it immediately. If they'd killed a person to show the horrors of eating meat, they'd have made sure the facts got out to the press without delay.

Sophie Gretzka turned up alive, living at Nicholas Lane's house. Sophie never intended to go to Florida with Gretzka. They were separating. In fact, besides feeling sick, that was another reason he wanted to take his vacation early. His marriage was failing and he needed to get away.

The day Serge Gretzka "left for Florida," Sophie moved out—and into Nicholas Lane's house. She didn't know Gretzka was missing until McCoo announced it on Tuesday at four. Until then, she assumed he was in Florida.

When she heard, she thought she might be accused. It's always the spouse who gets blamed for murder, she thought, especially when they're fighting. Sophie is flighty and, frankly, she's maybe not the sharpest knife in the drawer. Nicholas Lane is a great baker, and a hunk, but he's maybe not tops in the reasoning department, either. Basically they dithered for a day. They hadn't quite figured out what to do, although they say they were leaning toward telling the cops where she was, but the evening of the next day the Underhills were caught.

Sam and I had a quiet evening.

"Sam, I've been thinking. Part of the reason I've resisted the idea of marrying is that I was just so damn proud of myself. Living alone. Running my own life. I was Clint Eastwood, only very short."

He smiled. I loved that smile.

Did my heart lift when I saw him walk into a room? Yes. Did I see him instantly in a crowd, no matter how large and muddled? Yes.

What was I doing, "testing" a good man like Sam? A man I should feel lucky to count as my friend and suitor. How nasty and suspicious of me.

He passed the test, though.

EPILOGUE

From the simple to the complex. Two great recipes:

RITA RAK'S BUTTER COOKIES

1 lb. butter
1 cup sugar
2 egg yolks
1 tsp. vanilla
4 cups flour

Cream butter and sugar. Add egg yolks and vanilla. Gradually add flour. Roll out and cut with a cookie cutter or put through a sturdy cookie press. No need to grease the cookie sheet. Bake at 350 degrees about 10 to 12 minutes.

Deceptively simple, this cookie is simply delicious. It can be varied by adding grated lemon peel or orange peel, but you really don't need to gild this lily. Because it is a stiff dough, it can be formed into wreaths or other shapes for holidays.

From *Notes on Food* by Bruno Angelotti:

Osso buco is a specialty of Milan, in Lombardy, the northernmost part of Italy, where you find beautiful, serene Lake Como. The origins of *osso buco* are lost in the very distant past, but it can be traced as far back as the twelfth century in very much its present form.

Select from a display of veal shins several good, large bones with sufficient meat on them. Saw—do *not* chop or crack—the veal shinbones into two- to three-inch pieces. Tie the veal shin meat to the bones so that it will not fall off during cooking.

Chop carrots, onions, celery, and garlic. This mixture, before cooking, is called a *battuto.* Sauté in melted butter in a heavy casserole until the onions are transparent and the mass turns into a lightly browned *soffrito.*

Heat olive oil in a heavy skillet, but do not let it burn. Brown the meat and bones in the heavy skillet, turning constantly with tongs or a large spoon.

Place the vegetables in the casserole and carefully stand the veal shanks upright on top of them. Salt and pepper to taste.

Select several meaty tomatoes, preferably plum tomatoes, such as Roma or San

Marzano. Dip in boiling water for seven seconds. Peel, seed, and chop. Scatter the chopped tomatoes, basil, thyme, and cracked pepper over the meat in the casserole.

Heat white wine and beef stock sufficient to come halfway up the meat in the casserole.

Cover and bake at a temperature hot enough to maintain the liquid at a gentle simmer. Bake until the meat is fork-tender.

Chop parsley, garlic, and lemon peel. Mix one part of garlic and one part of lemon peel to three parts of parsley to make a *gremolata*.

Remove the bubbling casserole from the oven and turn the heat up to 450 degrees.

Transfer the bones carefully to an oven-proof dish, using tongs or a large spoon in order not to lose any meat or the marrow from the bones. Bake the veal bones in the hot oven for five to ten minutes until they are beautifully browned, but do not let them burn.

Strain the vegetables and the casserole juices through a fine strainer into a saucepan, pressing the juice out of the vegetables. Reduce the braising liquid to half its volume by boiling over high heat.

Remove the bones from the oven. Pour the reduced sauce over the shanks, for a shiny glaze. Sprinkle the top with the *gremolata*.

Serve with a special long, narrow spoon, designed to eat the marrow of the bones. Serve with risotto Milanese and a robust red wine.

ABOUT THE AUTHOR

In addition to her Cat Marsala series, Barbara D'Amato is the author of the Anthony- and Agatha-winning true crime book *The Doctor, the Murder, the Mystery: The True Story of the Dr. John Branion Murder Case,* as well as a mystery novel, *On My Honor,* which was nominated for an Anthony in 1990. Her musical comedies have been produced in London and Chicago. She is a past president of Sisters-in-Crime International and also of the Midwest chapter of Mystery Writers of America. She lives in Chicago, Illinois, and Holland, Michigan.

Ms. D'Amato recently won the Carl Sandburg Award for Literary Excellence in Fiction, 1998.